The Princess and the Evil Queen

LOLA ANDREWS

THE PRINCESS AND THE EVIL QUEEN

This book is a work of fiction. Names, characters, businesses, organizations, places, events and incidents either are the product of the author's imagination or are used fictitiously. Any resemblance to actual persons, living or dead, events, or locales is entirely coincidental.

For information contact:
https://www.lolaandrews.com

Cover design by VARVARA
ISBN: 9781094785561
First edition: April 2019

Once upon a time, there was a king. He was a cruel king, of handsome face yet harsh of hand, with a taste for conquest and lack of mercy, who exerted his power with the ease of one who dismisses everyone else's comfort.

Yet he was king, and for that, he was afforded power.

Noblemen feared him, but supported his conquering efforts as means of seeing their own riches grow; his army feared him as well, for lack of discipline was punished with death, but were loyal to his war campaigns and the glory of battle; the common people feared him too, and all they had was their fear, for they died of cold and hunger, and suffered in their flesh the excesses of the king's desires.

The king loved food, wine and blood, but nothing fired up his soul more than women, the youngest and prettiest doomed to fall prey to his wild appetites. It was well known among the villagers that daughter or wife could be claimed at any moment and made to be companion in the king's bed. Fathers hid their beautiful daughters away, chastised their wives if they dared let their hair loose or uncover their skin past their face and hands. And in fear women lived, too, for beauty was cause for punishment, and vanity the most terrible sin.

There came a day when two beautiful sisters were born. Twins they were, and handsome as the sun. Together they grew, happy, unawares under the jolly roof of their mother and father, farmers who had a hard life but who always had bread to put on their table, and hot broth to pass the harsh colds of winter. The family was loved by all at their village, and none more so than the two beautiful little girls, whose laughter brought joy to the most difficult of days.

Lily Rose and Marigold were their names, and indeed they looked like flowers. So beautiful and alike they were, and such taste they had for walking in the forest, that the rumors soon said that they had a touch of the fae. They did, for the faeries of old favored them, and often appeared to them as the girls strolled amongst the woods. The fae sang their song of old and played at placing light kisses on the girls' cheeks and hands.

The girls grew, and so did their beauty. Many warned their father to be wary of such gift, and most of all, of the envious hearts that wished them ill. Lily Rose and Marigold's parents had never known hate, and they couldn't understand why someone would ever envy them or wish to hurt them. They were good people, happy to lend a hand where it was needed and to offer a roof and warm soup to those who had none during the winter. They provoked envy, though, for they had a blissful and charmed life. And so it was that people of ugly hearts and ugly minds let their tongues run with the rumors that soon reached the king's ears.

The king heard of Lily Rose and Marigold during a time of peace, in which entertainment was but hunting and drinking wine. The king was bored without a battle to fight and with no woman to bed, so that claims of such beauty brought fire back to his chest. He took off that same afternoon, and he galloped through forests and dusty paths, past rivers and high mountains, and mounted on his favored steed, he arrived at a small village at the edge of his kingdom, where the beautiful girls dwelled in naïve comfort. Among screams they were torn from their home and their parents' loving embrace, and among cries they were taken to the royal palace, where they would become favored pets and enslaved companions.

The years passed, and despite the king's cruelty and abuse, Lily Rose and Marigold remained beautiful, exotic caged birds that the king admired and hurt with placid ease. The king took a wife, yet Lily Rose and Marigold remained his favorites, trapped in a tower, behind a set of heavy doors and guarded by his most loyal men, with only a window to see the world. Marigold withered as the days ticked by and the winters passed, and in her sadness, she was made more delicate, a porcelain doll ready to be broken. Of the two, it was her the king favored, for Lily Rose had grown angry with the years, and the king had learnt to fear the fire burning behind her eyes.

Lily Rose watched over her sister's spirit as best as she could, yet she didn't cry alongside her. She spent her days praying to the faeries of old, who had once upon a time kissed her cheeks and played with her hair as she walked through their fae woods. She prayed not for release but for revenge, and swore that she would pay whatever price the faeries asked for if only her wishes were met.

There came the day when Marigold perished, grief growing like a root around her heart and condemning her to die young and beautiful. Lily Rose looked upon her sister's dead body and was driven silent by pain. She longed for the days when they were children, and when Marigold's pale cheeks were rosy and filled with life. She cursed the king then, promised retribution fit for his crime, clawed at his face and claimed his blood with her nails. Tired of her, more fearful than he was doting, the king pushed Lily Rose away from his palace and his life, with nothing but her dress turned into rags to carry with her.

Alone and grieving, Lily Rose wandered, and soon found her feet taking her to the woods, where the fae spoke to her in song, and played with her hair, and kissed her fair cheeks and her soft hands. Following their song, Lily Rose found a secret grove where water flowed warm and flowers swam in the surface, and where birds sang amongst thick, green-leaved trees. Lily Rose bathed in the magical waters, and she felt as if she were washing a pain as old as herself. She slept on the soft grass, naked, and felt herself become part of the earth. And as she did, she dreamed of revenge.

The fae whispered in Lily Rose's ears, and soon she understood that they would help her, if only she paid the right price. The faeries dressed her in flowers and leaves, and she emerged as a nymph from the woods, her beauty crowned by sunrays and cleansed by water. She seduced the king's most trusted general, a man of strength, of square chin and bright eyes. She dragged him to the woods at the witching hour, and laid claim to his strength, his pride and his gumption under the full moon. Then, she made her offer to the fae, cutting the general's throat and letting his blood flow into the earth.

A babe was born; a baby girl so beautiful that Lily Rose's own beauty paled in comparison; a baby girl so beautiful that her beauty would become avenging fury. Her head was crowned by hair the color of burnt copper, and since she was born of blood and rage, she was named Harlow[1].

Harlow grew up in the forest, wild and free, cared for and loved by her mother and the fairies of old. She ate wild berries and slept under the open skies, and she tasted the freedom that her mother Lily Rose commanded her to cherish and enjoy, for it would not last forever. Harlow's destiny was fury and revenge, and so her mother told her as the winters passed and Harlow grew. Lily Rose bid her grow up strong and fierce, and as she dressed Harlow's dark red hair in flowers and bathed her skin in warm waters, she told of her sister Marigold and of the terrible destiny that had befallen her at the hands of a cruel king. She told of the promise the faeries had made, of Harlow's wretched father, and of the night Harlow was born under a full blood moon, a promise of punishment to come.

On her sixteenth birthday, Harlow emerged from the woods, dressed in flowers and leaves, as her mother once had. She bid her mother goodbye, and took comfort in the whispers of the fae, which followed her past the edges of the woods and guided her steps. She arrived at the palace's doors, and she was welcomed with surprise and fear both, for her beauty was grand yet foreign. Her hair shone like fire as it fell on wide waves down her back, her eyes were bright hazel and otherworldly, and her skin was tan, the color of gold. Upon seeing her, the king fell at her feet and promised to pray at her altar, for surely she must be a goddess.

---

[1] Name of English origin meaning "army".

The king barked orders for clean water and fine fabrics, and Harlow was spruced up prettily, her flowers and leaves left behind to rot. She allowed it even as she yearned for the freedom of the woods and the warm water of her mother's secret grove. She closed her eyes and begged for company. The faeries answered to the call of her blood and found a place to dwell behind the palace's mirrors, where they could whisper their secrets, which only Harlow would hear.

The king's wife had died years ago after a terrible illness, and since the king found himself in need of a new companion, he proudly announced to Harlow that she would have the honor. A fortnight passed while the wedding was prepared, during which Harlow prevailed upon the king's kindness and ordered him away from her bed until they were man and wife. So taken was he with her beauty and her spell that he complied, and so took to their wedding feast with fiery disposition and anticipation burning his loins.

Night fell, and under the glint of a full moon, the king found Harlow and forcibly claimed that which he had deemed his. Harlow sacrificed her virtue and her beauty to the king's cruel hands, and as he lay atop her, passion parting his lips, Harlow looked within her for the magic that was in her blood. She brought her hand to the king's chest, and with fury in her heart and revenge as her end, her fingers crossed nimble flesh and dug themselves inside the king, taking hold of his heart.

"Look at me, cruel king," she said, staring at the eyes above hers, at the old features of this cruel king that were now contorted in pain. "Look at me and fear me, for I was born to take revenge on your merciless evil, and to rain death upon you."

Such was the death of the cruel king, and upon his passing, so did Lily Rose die. Harlow felt it in her heart, a pain so gripping that it left her breathless, and that her whispering mirrors could not console.

Harlow thus cried during her ill-fated husband's wake, not for the king that had died by her hand, but for the mother that had left her alone in the world, with a new crown upon her head and nowhere to turn to. And as she cried, she felt a small hand take her own, a grip so strong that it surprised her. Harlow looked at the person by her side, and for the first time, laid eyes upon Snow White.

The king had had a wife, a young princess that had afforded him lands and riches upon marriage, and who had been as much a slave as Lily Rose and Marigold themselves. Sickly from childhood, a little feeble-minded and with a taste for books, she had been thrown into the northern tower of the palace, opposite where Lily Rose and Marigold had been enslaved. In her tower, the princess, made queen only in title, had looked at the cloudy skies of autumn and the clear ones of summer, and had dreamed of a better world. She had found it inside the pages of her books, and with them she had traveled without taking a step outside her tower. She too had forgotten of her husband's crimes, of the unkind hands he had laid upon her, and had escaped his merciless character through the pages that told of princesses and heroines, of spell and the power of true love.

Sick as she had been growing up, the queen hadn't expected to bear children, yet she had discovered herself pregnant during a wintry morning in which the sun had shone clear white rays through her window. She had smiled for the first time in years, and had cherished the life growing inside her. A baby girl had been born, of dark hair and pale skin, of lips so red that they had reminded the queen of spring poppies and summer skies. However, as she'd been conceived during bright winter days, the queen had named her Snow White.

Snow White had grown up in her mother's tower, amongst her books and her fantasies. She too had grown among the kindness of the servants, and running wild around the forests that surrounded the palace. She would often be seen running barefoot and careless, long dark hair free from ties and cheeks flushed with joy. She had laughter in her, and because of that the kingdom loved her, for her abandon was cheerful and easy to cherish. Most of her time was spent in the tower, though, where she read to her mother and heard the birds sing, where she weaved her own dreams to those of her mother, and wished for the day that she would escape this palace made of gloom.

The queen took ill upon Snow's tenth birthday. Forced into bed and unwilling to fight her fate, she consumed herself slowly, her mind leaving her body before life did so that she spoke of lands she had never visited, and of adventures she'd never lived. Snow took to her caring with faithful hands, and even as the queen blabbered in confusion, Snow read to her, and perched herself by their single window so she could speak of the days outside, the singing birds and the winds of winter. The queen died amongst fluffy pillows, her mind far away and her hand cradled inside her loving daughter's.

Snow grew moody after her mother's death, and found that stories could no longer take her away from her sad existence. Ignored by her father and neglected of care, she took to wandering the woods for days, and to spending her time surrounded by critters and birds. Sharp tongues condemned her for a lunatic, and it was said that she spoke to the animals and the wind, that she had a touch of magic. She was more loved than she was hated, though, for the queen had been sweet and undemanding, and Snow was as well.

Years passed, and at fourteen, Snow saw the king take a new wife. Snow watched the new queen during the wedding feast, her copper hair and her hazel eyes, her skin of gold and her fairy beauty, and she wondered if there was spell in her, and whether she was a creature of another world. Upon the king's death, however, and during his wake, Snow looked at the new queen once more and saw grief etched into her eyes, and saw that she was young, and lonely, and scared. Her spell was no less powerful for it, yet it was human and not otherworldly, and it softened Snow's heart. Snow took the new queen's hand, and when the queen looked down at her, she smiled.

"I am Snow White, Your Majesty," she said. "If you so wish, we shall become friends."

The queen blinked once, twice, as if surprised. Then, she smiled, and her smile was spellbinding as she said, "Let us wait and see, Princess Snow White."

Princess and queen both grew up together, and as they did, they grew apart. Fate thrust them in different directions, and as Snow grew kinder and loved by the kingdom, Harlow grew cruel and feared by her peers.

Harlow spoke to her mirrors, and soon she was called a witch. She was seen walking into the forest dressed in flowers and leaves, and the people spoke of evil spell and dark magic, of forces beyond their control. Harlow turned an angry heart to those who spoke ill of her, for darkness had taken root in her chest and she had no wish to fight it. She had been born of avenging desire, and now that her revenge had been exacted, she lacked direction and will both, and had only pain of old to hold on to. Thus, she took to potions and bewitchment, and looked for advice behind her whispering mirrors.

Nonetheless, she was queen, and now that the kingdom lacked its king, the noblemen turned to her for official business. Harlow took the offered power and made use of it with caution, knowing nothing of the world beyond her mother's secret grove. Advised by counselors and making use of books for knowledge, Harlow found a new world to love within the confines of her royal title. She became head of her army with gusto, head of her household with dutiful commitment, head of her council with aplomb, and head of her kingdom with agile intellect.

However so, her mirrors whispered and so did her kingdom, and both spoke of fear and ruin. Harlow's hand was decisive and true in her rule, and even when she fought hunger and cold, when she offered education and work, when she gave fair advice and just authority, she was deemed a witch, and thus unfit to rule. Stricken by grief and growing hard of heart, Harlow listened to her mirrors and found that they spoke truths that she didn't wish to hear – for so long as Snow White lived, the people would claim her as their true queen, and they would deny Harlow her rightful place.

Harlow's mirrors claimed Snow's blood, yet Harlow wavered. The princess was so kind, after all, and was so enthralled by Harlow, too. She sought her even now, when Harlow's temperament had turned harsh and unforgiving, when an aura of dangerous magic clung to her very being and scared even the most valiant of men away. Snow betrayed no fear, and in her naïve admiration, she stopped Harlow's hand from becoming deathly.

Years passed, and upon Snow's eighteenth birthday, a riot begun at the heart of the kingdom. The people claimed Snow as their true ruler, and they dismissed Harlow as witch and priestess of death. They called her the Evil Queen, and upon receiving such title, everyone forgot that she had ever had any other name.

Harlow took the name as if it were a gift and dressed herself in its power of legend. She became the Evil Queen, and in doing so, she left mercy behind. She listened to her mirrors, heard them speak of what was to be done, and made a harsh decision. The princess must die for the Evil Queen to reign free of burden, and so the royal huntsman was ordered to take the princess to the forest and to do away with her life. Her blood would flow into the earth, and become sacrifice to the faeries of old.

Snow had remained kind, and so it was that she called upon the huntsman's mercy and escaped her deathly fate. Relentless, the Evil Queen used her magic to dress herself as an old hag and poisoned the princess to sleep forever, a red apple her condemnation, and her naiveté to blame for her fall. It would not be the end of Snow White's story, for she was found by a handsome prince and soon awoken from the terrible spell, and made wife and princess again, by virtue of marriage.

Death was deemed the fair punishment for the Evil Queen; yet she was still queen, and head of her army, head of her household, head of her council and head of her kingdom. The queen's generals and noblemen were loyal to her, and so a war begun. A war of magic and blood, a war fought between the most beautiful women in the world, a war of terrible destiny and grim resolution. And it was thus, upon a rainy battlefield after years of war that a deal was struck. A deal between a princess and an Evil Queen, that would perhaps deny fate its claim for blood.

The Princess and the Evil Queen

The first drop of rain fell upon the ground before the hooves of Snow White's horse. The second one fell upon her skin, missing her leathers and armor and dripping down the back of her neck, upsettingly cold. She shivered, and as she looked up at the sky, rain finally started to fall over them, horses and soldiers alike.

"How fitting," the prince said next to her, a big smile on his face.

Snow smiled back reluctantly. Prince Charles, her husband, had a taste for drama that she didn't share. She was cold and uncomfortable, and this battlefield was the last place she wanted to be. She had no choice but to stand her ground, however, for Charles' enemy was, in fact, her own. The Evil Queen, or so everyone called her. Snow still had a hard time thinking of her as such, and in her thoughts, she remained Harlow.

"She's calling to us," Snow said, looking at the queen a few feet away, standing before her fierce army.

They too had an army at their backs, so that they could fight the final battle that would decide the fate of this years-long war. Charles had been saying as much for weeks now, but Snow held her doubts. They had been fighting for so long, had sacrificed so many lives to this conflict of old, yet Snow failed to see an end. Charles would not allow defeat, and Harlow would never surrender by her own will. Snow had never wanted to fight this war to begin with, but Charles had promised to defend her honor when they had married, and so far her honor seemed to comprise Harlow's lands and a claim of victory.

Together, Snow and Charles trotted towards the middle of the battlefield, as did the queen. She was wearing black, and Snow had the thought that it didn't suit her, and wished that her red hair was free of ties and falling loose about her shoulders.

"Let us end this conflict today," Harlow said once they were close enough. She had to shout her words to be heard above the sound of the rain hitting the ground.

Next to Snow, Charles laughed, a booming noise that startled her. "Yes, let us. Why don't we solve this in one battle? Your best man against me in single combat."

Harlow smiled, something small and sly, attractive beyond measure, and took her eyes away from Charles to look at Snow instead. "How quick men are to take this war away from our hands. Don't you think, dear Snow, that it should be us fighting this last battle?"

"You speak nonsense, wo–"

"But she's right, Charles!" Snow yelled, hoping for her voice to conquer her husband's and the rain both.

Charles looked at her with surprise written in his eyes. She so seldom had the strength to speak above him, or to make her opinion clear, after all.

"What do you propose we do, Your Majesty? Wield our swords in battle?" Snow questioned, amusement painting her words.

"We won't listen to whatever spell she plans to weave," Charles countered.

"Oh, do shut up," Harlow interrupted, waving her hand dismissively Charles' way and bewitching his voice away. Charles bristled visibly, but Snow had seen this spell before and knew that it didn't last long.

Looking at Harlow again, Snow had a hard time remembering that this was a woman of fury and battle before her. All she could see was her impish beauty and the charm she had always felt so enthralled by, even at fourteen. Harlow was making an effort to keep her spellbound, too, Snow knew, her hazel eyes unblinking and focused on her own, making of their locked gazes an intimate gesture. Held within Harlow's gaze, Snow could pretend that they weren't getting drenched in a muddied battlefield.

"We shall make a deal, you and I, Princess Snow," Harlow said, speaking her words as an enchantment, so that Snow couldn't doubt that they would indeed strike a deal.

Hugging herself as if to ward off the cold, Snow nodded, and muttered, "Name your terms."

Harlow couldn't have possibly heard her above the rain, yet she spoke as if she needed no words to know Snow's mind. "There is a full moon tonight," she said, and while Charles looked up for confirmation, Harlow and Snow didn't break their gazes away from each other, lest the spell be broken.

"You will come with me, Snow," the queen said next. "You will spend a moon cycle by my side, and attend my every request. Upon the next full moon, you will make a choice." Putting her hands up as if to weigh her own options, Harlow motioned towards Charles, and said, "Choose to leave and go back to your husband the prince, and I will vanish away forever." Then, motioning towards herself, she continued, "Choose to stay with me, and we shall end this war and leave our borders as they were, never to be crossed again."

Charles shook violently at that, anxiously pulling from his horse's reins and making it whinny, so that his protest would be acknowledged even if silenced by spell. Snow didn't need his words to understand his opposition, to know that he would gladly accuse Harlow of betraying the pact, or of causing her torturous harm were Snow to accept. He might be correct, too, yet Snow couldn't help but trust Harlow's words, for they were spoken candidly.

"Either way, there would be no more bloodshed," Snow said, thinking out loud, guessing that she had already made a decision, even if not entirely knowingly.

Perhaps, too, she longed to see the palace where she had grown up, the tower she had dwelled in with her mother for so many years, the court she had known well and the servants that had raised her. Charles' court had always felt so foreign, and their never-ending war had kept her from acquainting herself with the places and people, so that she was princess to a kingdom unknown.

"A truce shall rule our lands for as long as I remain by your side," Snow said then. "No battles, no more blood on either side; no more death and bones and dust."

"But of course," Harlow answered, her small smile widening, turning her plump lips deadly and alluring both. Yet her smile showed the small gap between her front teeth as well, which Snow had always thought charming, and which stole away from her aura of power.

Snow nodded, and then said, "Then we have a deal, Your Majesty."

Thus, Snow White and the Evil Queen trotted away from the rainy battlefield together, leaving behind a befuddled and silent prince, and claiming their truce without bloodshed and by mutual agreement.

The journey back to the palace took a little over two days, during which Harlow allowed for no stops. Snow was glad for it. The mindlessness of the ride stopped her from focusing on the twirling thoughts that were now assaulting her and making her question her choice.

By the time they arrived at the palace it had stopped raining, yet Snow felt chilled to the bone and very much like a drowned rat. She was sure she looked like one, too, so she was happy when she was silently ushered up the northern stairs and ordered to take a bath.

Climbing up the north tower of the palace, Snow couldn't help herself from taking off and running up the staircase. She felt full of energy despite the heavy weight of her wet riding leathers and armor. She couldn't wait to be back inside her mother's old rooms, where she had spent so many hours looking at the blue skies and dreaming amongst books.

Mother's bedchambers had been left untouched. Snow smiled candidly at Harlow's unwitting kindness, that she should leave this haven just as it had always been. Snow perched herself by the window immediately and looked outside at the cloudy sky. Then, she took a big, long breath, and felt a pang inside her chest, something like nostalgia clouding her senses.

She wasn't afforded time to rest and was instead quickly undressed and thrown into a tub full of warm water, which soon turned muddy. The water was changed and Snow remained speechless, letting old, familiar faces prod at her, clean her hair, rub the dust of the roads away from her skin. She wondered if she would ever wholly cleanse herself of the smell of war, the pervasive dusty scent of death, of tangy blood dried in the mud. Harlow had offered her a chance to do so, perhaps. She couldn't know, though, couldn't fathom what Harlow's true intentions were.

Harlow had always been mysterious, from the moment she had appeared at the palace, the vision of a nymph crawling from the forest, a creature of old, foreign and strange so that many had thought her but a dream. Snow hadn't been immune to her allure. Quite the contrary. She had craved her presence above all others and had strived to see her smile, the funny gap between her teeth and the shine behind her bewitching eyes.

Snow still remembered the nights of the winter solstice, during which there would be dancing around a bonfire built at the edge of the forest, plenty of wine and fruit and bread to pass around; during which the court had felt less like one and more like a coven of remote beings. Harlow had looked her most human then, and Snow had enjoyed curling herself next to her and insisting that they look up at the stars in the sky. Sitting close together, sharing their warmth and drinking from the same cup, Snow had never loved anyone more. Even now, the feeling was easy to evoke, and it burnt inside Snow's chest, pleasant and tender, yet painful. She shouldn't forget, after all, that Harlow had ordered her killed.

Snow left her bath at midday, when a shy sun was high up in the sky and warm rays filtered through the greying clouds. She was exhausted, weary now from years of battle, so she soon fell into a dreamless sleep.

Awoken by servants, Snow was surprised to find a gown selected for her to wear. It was one of her old dresses, one she had favored over the rest because of its lovely fabric, a soft pink taffeta patterned with big, white flowers, light and pretty. She had never felt more like a princess than wearing it, so she allowed herself to be dressed with delight. Her long hair, which she'd cut abruptly that very afternoon to shoulder-length, hating the heavy and tangled mass that it had become during the past months, she insisted on keeping loose so it curled around her cheeks in small waves. She adorned it with a dark pink satin ribbon, and as she walked down to the dining hall, she forgot about the war and felt young, and innocent, and so very happy.

Harlow offered Snow a place next to her on the high table and Snow dropped herself on it as if on a cloud. Harlow smiled at her, a closed-mouthed attractive curve to her lips, and Snow had the passing thought that Harlow was a lioness, ready to pounce, clad in deep reds and golds, her cleavage vertiginous and her elegant neck put on display.

"I am ever so glad we have this chance at a truce," Snow said after sitting down, leaning forward and closer to Harlow, unwittingly searching her eyes. "This terrible war has been a miserab–"

"Hush, now, Princess; I didn't bring you here to speak of war and ruin my dinner. Lord Manderly is about to share his boar story once again and I do so enjoy his foolishness."

Snow laughed, searching for Lord Manderly and catching sight of him on the other side of the room, indeed getting ready to stand up and tell the story he had been spinning repeatedly for many years now, and still asked for nonetheless. He always made such a fuss, and every time he shared his adventure, it became all the more grandiose, so that it had become a running joke among the court.

"I haven't thought of Lord Manderly in years," Snow confessed. "Last I heard, the boar was the size of a small horse and he killed it with a hunting knife."

Next to her, Harlow laughed as well, the sound crystal clear even as she tried to hide her effusiveness behind a goblet full of wine. "The knife is rusty these days, but I'm afraid the boar hasn't grown any larger."

"I do so hope there comes a day when he kills it with a spoon."

Harlow laughed yet again, and then made a point of touching her fingers softly to Snow's wrist to force her attention towards the dinner table before them. It wasn't as lavish as it would have been before the war, but it was certainly more of a luxury than she'd known in the last months of battle and grime. There was mutton, chestnut sauce, crisp-looking vegetables, and fruit for dessert, as well as those spongy ginger cakes she had always loved so much. Snow decided to enjoy her dinner and to ignore Harlow's dismissiveness, as laughter and cheer were offered in exchange. There would be time to discuss the circumstances of their opposition and the nagging notion of Harlow's desire to see her dead.

A dark and starless night had fallen around them by the time they left the dining hall, Snow following Harlow without a request being made. They hadn't had a chance for intimacy yet and Snow wondered whether the queen would be more forthcoming in her intentions once they were alone.

Thinking herself directed to the king's old bedchambers, Snow was surprised when Harlow's steps took them up the southern stairs instead, past the third floor and towards the high tower. She had never seen this part of the palace and had, in fact, thought it completely abandoned. It was not so, for soon they were crossing a heavy set of wooden doors, walking past a small hall and entering a set of chambers not unlike her mother's own. The towers were twins, so Snow shouldn't be surprised that the chambers were, too. She was, however, and she walked into the chambers tilting her head in fascination and secretly wanting to perch herself by the window, to see if the sky was the same color from this side of the palace.

"I have never seen these rooms," she said.

"I know."

Snow turned on the spot to look at Harlow, now gazing back at her from across the room. Harlow's lovely arms were naked and her eyes spoke of secret warmth, so that Snow suddenly felt as if she were a newlywed, anxious for what was to come. What a silly thought, when she was already married and had known the nervousness of being a virgin bride. She didn't remember it feeling quite like this, however, such tension-filled anticipation.

Snow looked about the room, trying to distract herself and ignore Harlow as she moved inside and closer, the swish of her dress betraying her stealth. The chamber was richly furnished, deep greens in almost every corner. It looked lived in, too, and she wondered whether this was Harlow's sanctuary, where she could be herself and not the evil queen that accusing tongues made her to be.

There were mirrors all over the walls, and a strikingly ornate one standing by the windows, as well. Snow knew the mirrors whispered in Harlow's ears, not because she had heard the rumors but because she had seen Harlow enthralled by them before, seeing beyond them and into a world that was hidden from everyone else. Shivering at the thought, she put it at the back of her mind and moved her attention to a large painting of two beautiful women hanging by the bed. The women looked just the same, but before Snow had time to wonder about them, her attention was pulled somewhere else.

"Come here, Snow," Harlow said, motioning towards her much as she had at the battlefield.

Snow gazed towards Harlow and then followed her instruction without much of a thought. Harlow was standing by the hearth now, and the fire casted shadows upon her tan skin. Snow wondered whether she would feel as hot as the fire itself.

Rather than stand too close, however, Snow bypassed the queen and sat atop the round table at the corner of the room. It was a bad habit that she had never grown out of and which even now drove most anyone at any court insane. It proved she was unfit to be a princess, it seemed, and Snow had always found the notion so silly. Harlow didn't chastise her, but she did smile as if she had expected Snow's antics.

"Tell me," Harlow said, walking her way and casting shadows as she did, encroaching her in the corner of the room and covering the light of the fire with her silhouette. "What news do you have of your new life? Do you enjoy being wife and princess? Well," Harlow drawled, amused, "queen, if your prince is to have his way."

Snow said nothing, distracted as she was by Harlow's sudden proximity, by Harlow's hands hovering above her knees and Harlow's body insinuating itself between her legs. Fleetingly, Snow had the thought that she hadn't spared a moment to miss her husband.

"Well?" Harlow prodded, keeping her eyes steady upon Snow's even as her hands landed delicately upon her knees, and pushed them to part around her.

"You said you didn't want to speak of the war," Snow complained, knowing that notions of her husband and the person she was now would only bring forth thoughts of the battlefield.

Harlow shrugged, and the slight movement pulled Snow's eyes to her shoulder, to the bronze skin and the constellation of freckles adorning it.

"I speak of your husband, nothing else."

"He's a good man," Snow said, strangely defensive.

There was no lie in her statement, for Prince Charles was indeed a good man and a good husband, as well. He was her hero, after all, the savior prince that had come to her aid when the woman now crowding her space had put her under a sleeping spell. He had no place inside this room, however, and the thought of him was uncomfortable, inadequate.

"He takes good care of you, then? Of his true love princess?" Harlow said, mocking, smiling impishly at the notion of the true love's kiss that rumors said had awoken Snow from her spell.

There had been no such kiss and surely Harlow knew, for she had cast the spell and poisoned the apple herself.

"He's a good man," Snow repeated, at a loss for words and not wanting to speak of Charles any longer.

Harlow laughed, a cruel tint to the sound and to the expression curling her lips and making her eyes shine. She was still the most beautiful creature Snow had ever laid eyes upon.

Harlow moved swiftly away and down, her hands taking hold of the hem of Snow's gown to push it up and past her knees, to the edge of her stockings.

"What? I–"

"Leave your hands upon the table, won't you, princess?"

Snow looked at her own hands, now hanging in the air between them, curled as if to blindly reach for an unknown hold. She did as she was told thoughtlessly, pressing them to the table by her sides, palms down and fingers curled about the edge, suddenly thankful that she'd been given an order. Harlow smiled when she complied and so did Snow, unwittingly, confused and excited both by the feeling of the pads of Harlow's fingers resting above her knees, casually missing the thin fabric of her stockings to settle on her skin instead. Snow felt slightly cold, but Harlow's fingers were hot, nearly scorching.

Harlow's fingers didn't stop there. Her hands climbed up past Snow's knees and over her thighs, pressing softly yet firmly, caressing the naked skin under her gown. Snow couldn't say that she didn't know what was happening, nor that it was unexpected. Yet her heart was beating hard inside her chest, the palpitating sensation building into her throat and muddling her senses. She licked her lips and left them parted once Harlow's hands stopped at the top of her thighs and changed their course to travel inwards.

"I don't–"

"You don't?"

Harlow's smile was pleasantly entertained. She drummed her fingers on the inside of Snow's thighs.

"Does your prince take good care of you?" Harlow repeated, making her question all the more explicit by allowing one of her hands to wander to the apex of Snow's thighs, to the mass of wiry hair covering her secrets.

Snow remained quiet, knowing herself flushed and out of her depth. She shook her head, and then she nodded. She wasn't sure there was a question for her to answer, but Harlow laughed, nonetheless.

"Yes? No?" Harlow mocked, leaning closer so that her skin looked even more enticing, her long, long neck, her rounded shoulders and her sharp collarbones, and most of all the beautiful swell of her breasts.

Harlow's hands were soft, and they remained so even as they rested firmly between Snow's thighs and pushed, so that Snow's legs parted wider and she was forced to cant her hips forward and closer to those very hands. Harlow's touch was careful, exploring, testing the waters of Snow's confusion. Snow knew what she wanted, yet she didn't dare give shape to the thought. She thought instead of the wet parting of the skin between her thighs, of the heat pulsating where Harlow still didn't dare touch. Her breathing was so harsh now, and she watched Harlow's eyes travel to her heaving chest with fascination.

Snow curled her hands tighter around the edge of the table, finding support there to scooch closer to Harlow's body, however impossible it seemed. Harlow was now entirely in her space, the wide skirts of her dress between Snow's legs, the fabric touching her skin in places, a rough contrast to Harlow's hands. Harlow's face was so very close, too, and Snow realized she wanted to kiss her, to reach up and untangle the tight coil of her hair, to run her fingers through the thick, red curls, and get lost in her scent. She didn't, though, keeping to her silent promise of leaving her hands upon the table.

Harlow answered to her moving hips and pressed her thumbs past her mound and to the sensitive skin of her outer lips, where the hair grew thinner and was already wet. She stopped short of moving past the final gates to Snow's insides, however, and leant forward so that Snow thought she was going to be kissed. Harlow's mouth remained a breath away, though, impossibly attractive, and frustrating when it curved into a knowing smile.

"You can say no," Harlow whispered, the hot puffs of her breath touching Snow's cheeks so that her words were a lingering caress against her heated-up skin.

Breathless, Snow's next question was strangled, "Can I?"

"Yes."

Snow shook her head, unsure of which question she was answering. She looked into Harlow's eyes, those pools of deep hazel that were gazing back at her and that were like beacons in the low firelight of the room.

"But I came here to serve you," Snow replied in a whisper, unsure of her thoughts yet quite sure of her statement.

"Say that again."

"I came here to serve you."

Harlow's smile was vibrant then, a thing of beauty. Given permission, she pushed her thumb past Snow's last barriers, engulfing it in the warmth of her core and painting an invisible line over her opening. Snow breathed out, a moan getting caught in her throat. Harlow parted Snow's lips gently, and making sure that Snow's eyes were following her every move, she brought her thumb up and into her own mouth. She hummed around it, carefully licking away at the taste.

"You do taste nice," she whispered.

Snow closed her eyes briefly, feeling flushed and embarrassed, if not ashamed. She was so affected by Harlow's touches, by her voice and the sight of her skin, by that hand of hers that was once again diving under her skirts to find her pussy and her most sensitive spots. Snow let herself get lost in the feeling. She rolled her hips closer to Harlow's prodding fingers, asking for more without daring to speak. Harlow seemed happy to provide, though, and soon her fingers were pushing inside her, two at a time and a little more than Snow was ready for.

Harlow worked her slowly, pushing her fingers in and out carefully, curling her knuckles and pushing her other hand to the warm clit between Snow's legs, her palm and then just the tip of her finger, experimenting as Snow's moans grew from breathy to loud, until the cadence of her hips started to take on a steady rhythm. Snow felt herself broken open before Harlow's wishes, her warm flesh contracting about her and wanting to swallow her up. She was dripping wet, her thighs now coated in her own juices. She'd never before known such a thing.

Harlow's pace was languid as she took her time, teasing at her, leaving her fingers to caress rather than to run to completion. Eventually, she reached back for Snow's ass and, pressing her hand to the supple skin, she pushed forward so that Snow was perched at the edge of the table, her weight supported only by Harlow's own body, her feet hanging close to the floor without quite touching it. Harlow pushed harder then, three fingers deep inside Snow now and using her own weight to drive herself knuckle deep and stay there.

Snow gasped, breath leaving her as pressure exploded inside her, pleasure traveling up her back and then down, settling on her chest and curling about her limbs, the center of her delight Harlow's deft fingers. Snow moved her hands up unwittingly, and upon noticing it, brought them back down on the table all too quickly, so that a smacking sound conquered the otherwise silent room. It startled her and made her open her eyes and look straight into Harlow's, those big ponds of light that were now darkened with desire.

"Easy, Snow," Harlow said, and her voice was a thin and careful trickle, flowing cool as water against Snow's hot face.

Harlow kissed her then. Not her mouth, which she avoided deftly, but her flushed and sweaty cheeks, and her jaw, and her neck. Harlow's mouth traveled down, leaving a trail of kisses behind, matching the uncoordinated rhythm of her fingers inside her and settling at her neck contentedly, mouthing at the skin there surely with the intention of leaving a mark. Snow would like it if it were so, she realized, to wear the mark of this terrible queen, who was friend and foe at once, and now ardent lover. She would wear her mark on her insides, too, for surely the void between her legs would forever yearn for Harlow's touch, now that it had tasted it.

Snow's pleasure built discreetly, following the meter of Harlow's caresses, of her fingers inside her and around her, of her mouth and tongue soothing the skin that her teeth had nibbled on before. Snow felt suspended in time, the past years a long-lost memory and the future the blind fantasy of the unknown. Were it possible that she could remain here for the rest of her life, she might choose to do so. She would stay inside Harlow's warm embrace, dangling on the edge of bliss and being denied the pleasure of the fall. She wouldn't be able to take it much longer, though, not with her trembling thighs and the running anticipation coursing through her body; not with her skin more sensitive by the second so that each of Harlow's kisses sent a jolt of burning heat down to her pussy; not when Harlow's hands were working her relentlessly now, clear goal in mind.

Harlow pushed her thumb against her clit, rubbed fiercely up and down, sliding her skin against the wetness coating Snow's flesh. Snow broke her silent promise and brought her hands up and around Harlow's upper arms, holding on to her and reveling in her cresting desire and in the peak of delight that made her toes curl inside her pretty slippers. She sighed quietly, her desire burning pleasantly between her legs and pulsating around Harlow's fingers.

Harlow stayed inside her as she came down from her high, her fingers tender on her clit and as they curled their way out of her. Slow as molasses, Harlow moved back, leaving the spaces of Snow's curves with one last kiss against the mark she'd left on her neck, one last lingering caress to her pussy, her mound, her thighs, her knees, so that Snow felt bereft of her as soon as she'd taken a step back. Flushed and still trembling with the after waves of pleasure, Snow let her mouth hang open and kept her legs parted, unwittingly hoping for Harlow to come back, to breach the distance separating them. Snow would kiss her then, and touch her, undress her and discover the beautiful mysteries of her golden skin, she would cherish their intimacy and cast their ugly past away. She did none of those things, however, and stayed there, watching Harlow move.

Harlow stepped further away, but before turning around and dismissing their encounter as a casual windfall, she brought her fingers up once again. Snow could hardly see them in the low firelight, but she knew they were shiny with her juices. Harlow brought them to her lips and past them, her pretty mouth parting around two of them and sucking the taste away with a contented hum.

"Better than wine," she said, and then shrugged, ending their moment together and leaving Snow to collect herself amidst hazy senses, trembling thighs and sweaty palms.

Harlow played her game of indifference, sitting by her vanity and taking great care in starting to undo her hair. Snow spied her through her mirror, and she hated the eerie figure she painted under the shadows of the low light. She saw the evil witch of legend now, the terrible queen that had cavorted with devilish creatures and had decided that she must have Snow's life.

"I suppose I shall leave you," Snow murmured, finally climbing down from the table and standing on unsteady feet.

Harlow turned towards her, her posture stiff and her smile guarded, her hands still busy with her hair. "You suppose well."

Snow wished to hear different, yet she would not beg for the attention that wasn't freely given. Instead, she asked, "May I spend my nights in my mother's old rooms? Would that be acceptable, or do you have the dungeons planned for me?"

"Don't be silly, dear Snow, do as you please," Harlow said, dismissive once again. "And do send my maid in on your way out; I have so many pins digging into my skull it's a wonder I'm still sane."

"I may help, if you'd like."

"You are sweet, but it is work unfit for a princess."

"Yet *that* you consider fit," Snow blurted out, motioning towards the table she had just abandoned.

Harlow wasn't looking at her, yet she didn't miss Snow's meaning, nor her sudden indignation. She gave it no time to fester or to become an argument, though. "You are starting to become annoying now. Do run along."

Snow followed Harlow's instructions, which this time forced distance in between them. She hurried past the wooden doors and down the stairs, and only stopped running once she was on her way to the top of the opposite tower, where she was to spend her days. She climbed the steps heavily, the past days of confusion catching up to her and weighing upon her shoulders heavily, as if physical bricks piling over her back. Not two days ago, she had been a princess and a wife, fighting a war that she didn't want in the name of a crown that she had no desire to wear. Nonetheless, she had known her place and her duties, to her husband and his kingdom both. Now, she was a prisoner under undiscovered circumstances, a princess made lover all too willingly and turned into a harlot under the queen's disregard. Worst of all was that she wouldn't have denied Harlow had she known she would be neglected, but rather would have cherished their moment all the more.

Snow finally found rest in her old bed, under the deep red quilt her mother had once embroidered with her name. She looked for the small letters sewn at one of the corners and touched the golden thread lovingly. She closed her eyes tightly, and prayed for sleep.

The days that followed were as confusing as they were pleasant, and Snow settled into the strange routine with abandon. She decided not to think about the implications of her imprisonment or about Harlow's intentions, and instead relished the familiarity of the palace and the people that inhabited it.

On the first day, she visited the kitchens where she was received with clipped fondness by Mrs. Agnes, the head of household. She had been responsible for her upbringing, and had been the one to care for the practical matters of her childhood since her mother had been unable.

"Now look what you've done with your hair, Your Highness," Mrs. Agnes exclaimed upon first seeing her, immediately reminding Snow of the severe affection the old woman had always bestowed upon her.

Soon, Snow had gone back her old routines and had come to spend her time dreaming away amongst her mother's books, looking at the sky outside as she sat by the window in her tower, and flitting about carelessly around the palace and the forest outside. She too had taken to following Harlow around when allowed to do so, and had partaken quietly in discussions of state. War was still a delicate matter, and even if this strange truce had given both sides time to breathe and recover, there was still a great deal to manage. Troops needed to be fed and clothed, and peace had to be enforced since many outside the palace's walls still called for blood. The harsh winter was too a matter of discussion, for Harlow feared the severe season would bring death to their doors.

Snow watched Harlow move about and speak to her advisors and her court. She watched her flirt shamelessly and speak her mind, her tongue quick and sharp, yet careful to never offend in irreparable ways. Harlow laughed openly, and she did it genuinely, conquering those about her with her gaiety and her beauty, playing at being queen. Snow was mesmerized by her, by her every move and the way she treated her kingdom as her playground, not carelessly yet enjoying herself. There was such ease to her, to the way she moved and laughed and made herself to be harmless. No one would have accused her of evilness within this palace, Snow was sure. Still, she knew she would be foolish to ignore the danger of Harlow, of her beauty and her magic, and of the power she held over her.

Nevertheless, Snow enjoyed looking at her. She marveled at her unaffectedness. Snow's mother-in-law would have thought Harlow inappropriate, for she believed a queen's manners should be stiff and contrived. She always sat on any chair with an air of painful imposition, turning her back most uncomfortably and keeping her neck ramrod straight, her lips set in a rictus of disapproval. She hadn't liked Snow one bit when Charles had brought her home and proclaimed her his future wife, and she hadn't learnt to like her any better in the passing years. Snow had always guessed that her innate awkwardness had much to do with it, for she had none of Harlow's spontaneous grace and was instead clumsy and careless, with a taste for walking without her shoes and sitting atop tables. Charles often said that his mother only resented Snow's aloofness, which he himself liked so much.

"You are my princess, my magical princess," he would say, thinking her peculiarities a sign of her legendary touch of spell.

The truth of the matter was that Snow hadn't been raised as a proper princess, and she'd never had a natural inclination towards artificial mannerisms. She would have hoped for Charles to love her despite it, and to shed away the silly notions of the rumors of magic surrounding her.

Snow found that she didn't like thinking about Charles – not when she'd so willingly fallen into Harlow's embrace. She couldn't help herself from thoughts of him at night, though, when sweet winter wind touched her overheated skin and her very being was still hankering for Harlow's touch. She'd never felt such passion, after all, not when she'd had so little time to explore her intimacy with Charles, their marriage clouded by the shadows of the war. Snow didn't dislike Charles' touch, but she had never learned to enjoy it.

Her nightly encounters with Harlow had become a common occurrence and, despite her best efforts, Snow craved them. Harlow drove her crazy. Snow promised herself every night that she would deny her, but she was hard-pressed to do so when she was often wet even before Harlow had laid a hand upon her. Harlow would flirt of course, making her laugh during dinner, touching the inside of her wrist with firm fingers, curling them about her and reminding her of what they could do when buried inside her; she would hide a pleased little smile as she poured wine for Snow and encouraged her to enjoy the flavors of her table. Harlow prepared her for indulgence, so that every night, when she posed her silent offer, Snow followed her into her rooms and inevitably fell under her spell.

Harlow always did offer, which only made Snow feel guilty for being such an easy victim to her own passion. Had she been treated like a prisoner and forced into the queen's bed, then surely she would have run back to Charles free of blame. She was to blame, however, for she wanted Harlow and she didn't know how to deny herself the pleasure she offered behind the closed doors of her bedchambers.

One sunny afternoon found Snow taking a slow stroll through the forest, carefully bundled in her old winter coat and fighting the urge to slip out of her boots and touch her soles to the cold ground. It was cold but not humid, and under the weak rays the midday sun, she could pretend that it was warm. She walked over the stone bridge that crossed a small, nearby river, and took mindless steps towards the heart of the forest, towards where she remembered a clearing she had once favored. She found it after a time and sat down on a fallen tree trunk, content to surround herself with the fresh scent of winter and the earthy smell of moss. She felt at peace here, much more so than back at the palace or at Charles' own.

Soft breeze blew through the winter trees and Snow closed her eyes and enjoyed the fantasy of freedom. She wondered whether she would choose this existence, this penitence of pleasure next to a woman she cared for but couldn't understand, a woman that burned hot and cold and who had once longed for her death.

Thus entertained, she was caught by surprise by a ruffling noise not far away, on the opposite side of the clearing. She opened her eyes and looked for the origin of the disturbance. Harlow appeared before her, a vision as she stepped from the thickest of trees, so uncanny in her lure that Snow thought her a creature of the woods. Unconcerned with the cold, Harlow was clad in a thin tunic, her arms and shoulders bare and her dark red hair falling over them, her thick curls free of ties.

Upon seeing Snow, Harlow smiled, the curve of her lips enticing in its obvious delight. "We had the same thought," she said once she had walked the steps that separated them. She looked so very pleased that she seemed like a child before Snow's eyes.

"Aren't you cold?" Snow asked, her eyes sweeping over Harlow's arms, her neck and the soft collar of her tunic, riding low so that one more inch would allow her to take a peek at Harlow's nipples. How Snow wished she could spy their color.

Harlow laughed as she plunked herself next to her on the tree trunk, graceful even in her inelegance. "I'm always warm in the forest."

Snow looked into Harlow's eyes, and she would swear they twinkled with something like magic. She was smiling still and she looked like an imp, mischievous and youthful, the gap between her front teeth charming. As they stared at each other, Snow bewitched by the vision before her, Harlow grasped her hand unceremoniously and dragged it to her lap and then her mouth. She pressed her soft mouth to Snow's knuckles, half-closing her eyes as she kissed her skin reverently. Her kisses were silky, barely-there caresses that traveled to Snow's open palm and the inside of her wrist, and then back to her knuckles and the tips of her fingers. Snow licked her dry lips and then smiled, wistfully thinking of a future where this was her everyday life – walking the forest together, and kisses, lots of kisses everywhere. The choice was hers to make, but she would rather not think about the consequences of leaving her husband behind, and of surrendering completely to the mysteries of Harlow.

Wishing for reprieve from her confusion, Snow said, "I thought there were no paths beyond those trees, that there was just impenetrable wildness."

"These forests hold no secrets from me," Harlow answered, sparing her skin a moment to hold her gaze instead. It didn't last long and soon her lips were back upon Snow's palm, kissing more insistently now, with intention.

"I didn't think they held many for me, either," Snow said, pulling her hand away from Harlow's tempting mouth before she allowed herself to be too distracted.

Harlow hummed her disapproval, pulling Snow's hand back with childish stubbornness and keeping it on her lap as if proof of her command. She furrowed her brow and silently inquired about the meaning behind Snow's words.

"I suppose I believed there weren't very many secrets left once I'd spent a night running through the trees and scared for my life."

Snow left her words linger, soft so that they were not accusing. She'd been so afraid that night years ago, with the woods casting dark shadows above her and the glint of the huntsman's knife still a fresh memory. She had run even after the huntsman had promised mercy. Every sound and shape had frightened her in the darkness of the night. Daylight had brought reprieve, but it hadn't dissipated her confusion or the grief clouding her heart.

Harlow's expression was undecipherable, but she was looking at Snow with determination, not hiding from the guilt of her murderous acts, if she had any at all. She hadn't let go of Snow's hand and she was touching it carefully even now, her fingers rubbing circles on Snow's knuckles.

Harlow parted her lips and closed them again quickly as if unsure. She swallowed hard and tried once more. "Would you believe me if I were to tell you that I never meant you any harm? Not truly, not with malice, or–" Harlow interrupted herself, looked down at Snow's hand in between hers. "But it would be foolish to try and explain."

"No, it would not! Do tell me, please; help me understand what went on, what is going on even now, what you wa–"

Harlow interrupted her with an unexpected kiss, quieting her protests with plump, insistent lips above hers. They hadn't kissed before this moment and Snow yielded unashamedly, moaning when their lips first met and closing her eyes swiftly. Harlow's first approach was harsh, her wish to prevent Snow's pleas obvious in her tactic. However, as quickly as Snow had surrendered, so did Harlow relent, making the kiss into a tender caress. Harlow played with her mouth, trapping her upper lip and then breaking away, laughing breathily in between them at Snow's quiet whine and diving back in for a more forceful, passionate kiss. Snow parted her lips under Harlow's and Harlow ravished her, bringing her hands up around her cheeks and cupping her face so as to keep her in place. Her hands were warm and they burned against Snow's skin, flushed from the cold.

Snow moved to accommodate Harlow's silent requests, caressing her tongue as it delved inside her mouth and chasing it when it went away. Harlow always came back to her, making love to Snow's mouth with her tongue the same way she had to her pussy last night. Snow moaned, thinking of what Harlow could do to her, what she was doing to her already.

Harlow moved back and when Snow followed, she avoided her long enough to whisper in between their mouths, "You can touch me, if you'd like."

Snow took the opportunity with a groan, meeting Harlow's lips once again and reaching up to bury her hands between Harlow's loose curls as she'd been wanting to do for so long. She clung to her, the feeling of her thick curls weaved between her fingers and of her lips above hers impossibly intimate. Warmth pooled with placid ease between her thighs. She wanted Harlow to touch her further, but she wasn't willing to give up their kisses, the feeling too precious.

They did break apart, but only once the midday sun had waned and darkness was starting to set, making the cold biting. Harlow's lips were bruised by their kissing and Snow could only guess that hers much more so, her pale skin so easy to mark.

"I do like this," Harlow said once she'd taken a steadying breath, combing her fingers through Snow's short hair and wrapping a curl around her thumb.

"Mrs. Agnes was ever so upset that I'd cut it," Snow answered, shrugging and feeling suddenly timid under the intensity of Harlow's soft gaze. "It was terribly damaged, though."

"I think it suits you and besides, upsetting Mrs. Agnes is hardly an accomplishment. I do so at least once a day."

They took off together. Snow felt giddy, young and in love and a little stupid, making her imprisonment into a romantic tale. It was neither one nor the other, she knew, for things were never simple in Harlow's world. Nonetheless, she loved the forest and she loved their intimacy, the way Harlow had kissed her and the way she'd moaned against her mouth when Snow had dared cup her breasts, eager and inexperienced.

Harlow offered her hand as they walked and Snow slid her own into the proffered hold, marveling still at the warmth of Harlow's skin. They walked slowly, strolling through the dense parts of the forest with quiet regard, silent but together, holding onto one another and putting off their return.

Snow thought of Harlow as they walked, and of that one night years ago when she'd caught her in the throes of passion with another woman. Back then, Harlow had still inhabited the king's old bedchambers, rather than the southern tower, and Snow had had the most terrible habit of invading her privacy without much of a second thought. She'd been very young at the time, desperate to forge a friendship with the new queen and unaware of herself most of the time. Therefore, she hadn't thought twice about looking for Harlow in the middle of the night after a presentation ball, happy as she'd been after the feast, the light and the music, and having the majority of the court visiting the palace and breaking the everyday gloom that had pervaded the place while the king was alive. Harlow hadn't been alone upon Snow's arrival, and had in fact been entirely too preoccupied with someone else to even notice her presence. Snow had hidden by the chamber's doors, behind the light blue curtains adorning the frame, and had watched Harlow between the legs of a lady of the court. The woman had had her legs spread on the bed and her body had been taut, breasts bouncing with her panting, head thrown back and long hair undone over the pillow. Snow had stayed long enough to watch Harlow smile as the woman moaned in pleasure. She'd never quite forgotten about that night, and even now, she wondered how many women had shared Harlow's bed and how many had been allowed to offer pleasure in return. Snow had yet to be granted permission to touch, her sneaky hands this afternoon being the only allowance Harlow had made in that regard.

At last they made it back, and as soon as they lost the cover of the last trees, Harlow dropped Snow's hand and hugged her arms around herself as if the cold of the late afternoon had finally caught up with her. Snow laughed and took the liberty of reaching forward and rubbing her hands up and down Harlow's arms, hoping to offer warmth. Harlow allowed the brief touch, but soon took a step back and away from Snow, an awkward, tight-lipped smile darkening her features.

A member of the queen's guard awaited them at the edge of the forest, and upon seeing Harlow's discomfort, he came closer and offered her a winter coat. Harlow donned it gratefully and then proceeded at a brisk pace, leaving behind the contentment of the woods and turning back into her usual regal figure. Snow followed behind her, made curious by the figures of the Law and Military

Advisor, both men standing by the palace's main entrance in a waiting disposition. They were Harlow's most trusted allies and they genuinely favored her and her ruling hand. They had kept their distance from Snow out of deference to the queen and they had yet to speak to her.

This time, however, Snow's presence wasn't a deterrent for their words. Both men, agitated as they were, failed at conveying their message quickly and instead fumbled about, interrupting each other until Harlow shushed them both and ordered them to speak clearly.

"It is Prince Charles, Your Majesty," the Law Advisor said. "He's been seen foraying into the kingdom with a legion of a hundred at least. We believe he is making his way towards the palace in order to–"

"Valiantly rescue his princess, never mind our truce? Of course he would." This Harlow said in a clipped tone, anger shaping her mouth into an unkind and tense expression. Her eyes, too, seemed to change altogether in an instant and suddenly, Snow realized that she was staring at the unforgiving gait of the Evil Queen.

Snow believed what she hadn't quite grasped until then – that this woman had orchestrated her death; that, upon her failure, she had selected the ripest apple from her orchard and had poisoned it so as to fool her into a most terrible spell.

Snow wanted to look away. She didn't, and instead forced herself to see Harlow for who she was, all of her, dark now when she had been light only seconds before. She thought of the forest and wished for them to go back to the safe cover of the trees, where they'd been lovingly intimate and untouched by the war that separated them. Harlow didn't give her the privilege of ignorance, though, and she didn't even grace her with any attention. Instead, she walked into the palace, Snow following behind in hurried steps along with both advisors.

They made their way into the mirror chamber, a little awkward band of followers fearing the temperament of their queen. The chamber was shrouded in darkness and the waning sun crowding its way inside through the cracks of the heavy drapes casted strange shadows, caught in the many mirrors covering the walls and reflecting back into one another. The eerie glow of their reflections persecuted Snow wherever she looked and she hated that, in this chamber, she couldn't possibly escape Harlow and her terrifying eyes, her rigid severity. Their eyes met, a million looking glasses in between them and Snow not truly knowing where she was looking at, what or who she was seeing, whether it was Harlow before her or the reflection of a thousand mirrors pulling them apart. Snow was terrified, the feeling creeping up on her slowly, crawling up her spine in spidery discomfort and settling high up inside her chest. It felt scratchy, unwanted. She didn't want to be scared, she didn't want to look into the eyes of the Evil Queen, but still, she wouldn't look away.

Harlow broke their encounter, dismissive of Snow's anguish or perhaps subjugated under her own anger. She turned towards a favored mirror and her reflection was gigantic, horrifying, made of darkness, of spell and nightmares.

"Show me," Harlow commanded.

The surface of the mirror changed before Snow's incredulous eyes, allowing her to see the world behind it, those gates that Harlow could speak to and control. The crystal shifted like water, fluid and ever-changing until it stopped in a living picture. Snow saw the woods and she saw her husband, confidently ordering his men to set up camp for the night. It was a familiar sight, Charles' proud demeanor that didn't stop him from lending a hand, his kindness overshadowed only by the excess of confidence that Snow had often resented. He never listened. He thought he knew better and of course he would disregard Snow's silent request to allow her pact with Harlow to succeed. Briefly, unwittingly, Snow hated him for his self-righteousness.

"I should kill them all," Harlow said suddenly, leaning forward towards the mirror and touching its surface gingerly, right over Charles' chest, over his heart. "I *could* kill them all."

"No!" Snow exclaimed, pulling herself out of the trance of the mirror's spell and turning fully towards Harlow, searching her eyes and failing to catch them.

Harlow paid her no mind, nor both fumbling advisors, their voices once again struggling to find the right words and blending together in a confusing speech. She seemed trapped by her own contemplation, her own spell. Snow fought her bewitchment and walked forward, fearing that Harlow's hand, still poised over Charles' heart, would be deadly.

"Stop! Whatever it is you are doing, stop!"

Snow grabbed at Harlow's arm, dug her nails into the fabric of her coat and pulled at her, breaking her away from the mirror. The image shimmered away as soon as Harlow's eyes were distracted and she growled, tugging sharply and freeing herself from Snow's hold. She looked wild, and she turned towards Snow with bared teeth.

"You'd protect him? He broke his truce! He means to walk into my kingdom and be left unpunished!"

"He means no harm, he's on–"

"Oh, don't be foolish, Snow. He would run his sword through my heart if he could! He probably means to do so in the name of your virtue and my evilness. I might as well prove him right." Harlow turned towards the mirror once again and the magical image brightened up the obscured surface, now bringing sound with it, the cacophonous noise of men of battle resting for the day, laughing amidst the sound of clinging swords, rusty armor and a lonely, dissonant viol.

Once more, Snow reached out for Harlow's arm, intending to stop her anger however she could. Harlow avoided her, moving sharply away.

"Please," Snow begged, bringing her hands together and to her chest in anguish, now more than ever fearing what Harlow was doing to herself in her fury, what she would do to others. "Please, do not kill, *cariño*, please don't believe the voices that call you evil. You know better than them; *I* know better than them."

"Oh, I won't kill anyone," Harlow assured, sneering as she looked at Snow, probably thinking her pathetic for begging and for showing how much she cared. "At least, my hand won't."

Harlow's eyes shone golden, magic hidden in their depths and stripping them of beauty. She was a creature of old then, and when she stalked back towards her mirror, her gait was that of an ancient animal, a goddess prowling the earth and looking for her next victim. She spoke and her voice was deep, weaving spell and bewitching the world around her.

"Send them rain," she sang with her profound voice, casting the sorcery that would bend the elements to her whims. "Send them rain so harsh that their boots can't move over the mud. Send them hail, send them thunder and fire. Send them fear from the cloudy skies and let them know that a goddess is paying their betrayal with fury. Send them rain."

Thunder cracked far away where Charles' camp rested, yet Snow felt it inside her chest, booming with sound. She watched the mirror before her, looked at the skies turn grey, at the clouds gather above the camp. It rained, and it was angry rain, furious as Harlow was, cutting and unforgiving. The scent of the far-off storm pervaded the mirror room, invaded it as if it was inside it. It smelled deceptively nice, fresh and sweet, evocative and luxurious. The picture before her denied her the pleasure of believing the fantasy, though, for soon droplets of water became hailstones and began destroying the haphazard construction of the camp. Chaos ran free then, and all Snow could see was men screaming, gathering possessions amongst the deafening noise, looking for refuge yet afraid of the thunder, ever-closer now and threatening when falling close to the trees.

"Oh, Harlow…" Snow said, begging with her lingering words and her broken tone.

Snow looked away from the image before her, took a deep breath and held it in so as not to catch the deceitful scent of clean rain. She found Harlow's eyes and in them she found magic.

"Don't you dare look away, Snow White," Harlow declared. "Watch your prince's panic and suffer with him if you must. Don't you dare move a muscle, don't you dare."

Harlow set forth such words as if still casting her spell, and they had the effect of constraining magic in Snow. Harlow left the room and so did her advisors, yet Snow remained, standing before the terrible mirror and watching men fight the elements. Blood soon flowed before her eyes, hail blowing with more ferocity every moment and stones finding unguarded skin. The soldiers ran, leaving their weapons behind and searching for shelter, yet failing to move fast when their boots sunk into the mud, the slippery ground seeming like hands wanting to grab at them.

Snow remained standing for hours on end, feeling her own muscles burn and her limbs turn heavy, her frame asking her for respite. She didn't move, however, and she didn't close her eyes. She watched the thunderstorm approach, saw fire sprout from the woods, burn tents and clothes, catch a few soldiers unawares. She watched them scream as fire licked at their skin and she watched them pray for reprieve from the gods' above. Snow prayed too, not to faceless gods but to an angry queen, to her heart that Snow knew had good in it. For hours she watched, and upon looking at Charles' figure, proud stance and unwavering voice, blood pouring from a wound on his temple, she hated him. She hated his pride and his thoughtlessness, she hated his spirit that had demanded this war in the name of Snow's honor when she had never wanted such a thing.

But she hated Harlow, too, for her distance and her mystery and her cruelty. She hated her for denying that she could ever be good, that she could ever answer Charles' defiance with something other than equal fury.

Hours passed and the mirror shimmered again, erasing the image as the storm started to recede, the spell giving way to a tranquil night. Soon, the room was shrouded in darkness, Snow's reflection in the looking glass no more than a shadow, hunched, defeated and dark. The scent of the rain lingered, misleading her senses into a state of calm. She fell to her knees, tired, ever so tired, and pressed the heel of her hands to her eyes, dry tears making them itchy.

Quick steps invaded the room. Snow didn't look up nor did she move, but she felt someone kneeling by her and soft, desperate touches finding her hair, her cheek, her temple. Nervous hands prodded at her and soon they were joined by kisses, cold lips against her heated up skin a balm to her overwhelmed senses.

"I am so sorry, I am ever so sorry," she heard, and it was Harlow whispering quiet words, soothing her with them and surrounding her in this sudden, treacherous warmth.

Snow fought Harlow's hold without much success. A cold goblet was pressed against her lips and she drank. Her lips were ever so dry and her throat so tight that she choked in her anxiousness to taste the cool water.

"Slow down now, please, I–" Harlow murmured, still pressing sweet kisses to her temple, carding her fingers through her hair.

Harlow had brought one of her guards with her and she ordered him to carry Snow up the southern tower. Snow rejected the man, refusing to be made into a weak creature unable to take her own steps. She did allow him to support her as she walked because she felt dizzy and unfocused, the shadows of the palace darkened by the night confusing her tired senses.

The guard helped her all the way to Harlow's bed. He departed, and she was left alone with Harlow. She was too tired to hold on to her anger and, laying down on Harlow's big bed now, she wished for company and for mindless rest. There would be time to think tomorrow.

Harlow didn't come to her, but rather remained in front of her vanity mirror, looking past the dark surface and into the world that only she could see. She was pacing before it, anguished, grabbing at her loose hair and mumbling incomprehensible words, arguing with invisible forces. She looked mad, stripped of her power of old and made into a lunatic, desperate before whatever it was that she was hearing.

"I hate your mirrors," Snow said, her voice sounding croaky, ugly. "They're ever so eerie."

Harlow turned to look at her, and her gaze was soft. Her eyes looked red in the low light of the room, touched by unshed tears. Sniffling, she said, "Tonight, they are."

Harlow found a blanket somewhere in the room and threw it over the tallest mirror, taking its power away for the night. Then, she walked towards the bed and sat by Snow. She stared at her for long minutes and Snow stared back, blinking her tiredness away and wishing that the world could reduce itself to this – Harlow's concerned eyes shining with emotion and a bed for them to share. Harlow said nothing and Snow didn't either, fearing that her words would be accusing.

After a time, Harlow brought her hands to Snow's chest and begun undressing her. She was still wearing her winter coat and her heavy dress, so Harlow undid laces and buttons for a long time. Snow allowed herself to be moved this way and that when needed, and soon her coat was discarded and Harlow's hands were busy loosening up her corset and pulling her skirts down and away. Harlow's touch became more tender the closer she found herself to Snow's skin, so that she removed her stockings with reverence, the pads of her fingers ticklish and soft as they pulled the fabric down her thighs, past her knees, over her ankles and finally away from her feet. Harlow kissed her ankle sweetly, tickled the sole of her foot and smiled against her skin when Snow couldn't avoid a tired giggle.

Harlow pushed her hands under her shift in order to remove it, bringing it up past her knees and touching her as by accident, her hands phantom touches that brushed carefully against Snow. Snow helped, moving her hips up from the bed so the fabric could surpass her belly, arching her back and raising her arms up so that her shoulders and neck could be free. Harlow stopped once the thin fabric was bunched around Snow's wrists, her hands tangled with it as she held Snow's arms above her head. The position forced Harlow to lean over Snow's naked body and as she did, Snow noticed that her breathing was labored, hot puffs of air falling sweetly against her cheek.

Harlow's hair fell down by her sides and with them being so close, the rest of the world truly did feel faraway and foreign, an interruption to the intimacy of their romance. Snow parted her lips and Harlow's warm breath fell in between them. Harlow moved her hands down, leaving the fabric behind so that Snow remained still, as if truly tied down. Harlow's hands caressed her arms, her thumb pressing at the inside of her elbow, drawing a line all the way down to her shoulders, her collarbones and the swell of her breasts. She didn't cup them, but merely drew their contour with the tips of her fingers, ticklish once more as she played with the underside, teasing Snow's skin, raising goose bumps.

Snow took a deep, shaky breath when Harlow settled her palms over the plains of her stomach, unmoving yet firm, cooling down her skin. She felt as if her chest was about to explode.

"Why are you crying, dear Snow?" Harlow murmured, bringing cold lips to her fevered cheeks and taking away the tears that Snow hadn't realized where running down her face. "Please, don't, please, please, darling princess. I am ever so sorry, ever so…"

Harlow's litany continued, a yearning prayer of sorts, not devoid of magic. The candlelight flickered, yet Snow could see nothing but Harlow's eyes, the skin of her face as she came closer, her red hair surrounding her. She could feel nothing else and hear nothing else, so she closed her eyes and let herself fall into the spell of Harlow's hands over her belly, of her lips kissing her everywhere, sweet and kind and reverent, of her murmurs of repentance, of her trembling voice and her silent promises. She heard nothing more, felt nothing more, saw nothing more, and with Harlow claiming her very being, she succumbed to tiredness, and fell asleep.

Snow was wakened by the warm feeling of the sun against her face. She opened her eyes lazily, stretching under the covers while pondering whether to go back to sleep. The bed was warm and the linens smelled of the flowery perfume of Harlow's hair. She was tired still, too. Hunger won over laziness eventually, her stomach grumbling until she was too awake to insist on ignoring the high midday sun. She left the bed and upon finding a discarded robe, she covered her nudity with it, Harlow's scent enveloping her once more even away from her comfortable bed. It was a little long on her, but it settled nicely on her shoulders, the fabric sensually soft on her skin. She curled her toes and thought of Harlow's hands resting on her belly.

Her stomach complained once more, so she rang the bell next to the bed. It didn't take long for a chambermaid to come into the room carrying a heavy breakfast tray.

"Her Majesty guessed you would be hungry, Your Highness."

Snow smiled and looked at the tray loaded with warm bread, fresh fruits, salted meats and honeyed wine. A red apple rested amongst a bunch of beautiful purple grapes and shiny slices of orange, and Snow looked at it and wondered if Harlow had chosen this breakfast herself. If she had, then it was a cruel joke to add the apple to the otherwise wonderful meal.

She took the piece of fruit and offered it to the chambermaid. “Please take this,” she requested.

“Oh,” the maid said, her pretty cheeks flushing pink upon looking at the fruit. “Cook thought you might like one; the crop has been so tasty this year, you see. We didn’t think, I suppose. Please don’t mind it, Your Highness, there was no mockery behind the thought.”

“It’s quite all right, don’t fret.”

The girl smiled at her, and said, “The queen would hate for you to be uncomfortable.”

She curtsied when Snow nodded and, as she was about to leave the room, Snow had a sudden thought and asked, “Are you afraid of her?”

The girl turned towards her once more. Her cheeks were still flushed and at the mention of the queen, they only grew brighter. Snow wondered at that, thought that perhaps the palace was abuzz with rumors of hers and Harlow’s affair.

“Your Highness?”

“The queen, I mean. Are you afraid of her?”

“Oh no, Your Highness. Well… I suppose her magic… But then she’s always been kind to me. She took me in when no one would give me work, you see.”

“How come?”

The girl looked down, fidgeted uncomfortably for a moment so that Snow was tempted to stop her questions and let her go. However, the girl was quicker in her answer and confessed, “I have my little boy, and he has no father. Or, well, his father was never my husband and I was condemned to poverty and exclusion and she–"

The girl said no more, but when she looked up, her eyes were shiny and her lips were holding in a tight smile. Snow walked to her and held her hand about the girl's clasped ones, squeezing carefully. She sent her away with the apple and after having given her a long drink of wine, reassuring her that her story wouldn't run among sharps tongues any further, and that she would be glad to count her among the palace's staff.

Once the girl was gone, Snow kept on smiling. She felt giddy and she celebrated her bizarre mood by generously spreading jam over her bread and eating with gusto. She took the grapes when she was done and munched on them as she walked about the room, Harlow's robe still her only piece of clothing and her feet naked against the stone floor. She flipped over the books she found here and there, rested by Harlow's vanity for a moment, ignoring her messy hair and playing around with Harlow's perfumes, choosing one at random and dashing a few drops on her neck. Then, she spent a long while staring at the painting by the bed, those two strange women looking back at her as if they were alive under the colorful pigments. They were so very similar, yet at the same time so clearly different women that Snow found herself fascinated by them both. Her eyes were most drawn to the figure on the left, for her beauty hid such anger, such pain.

The late afternoon found her sitting by the windowsill and staring at the waning sun. It painted the sky dark orange and it was ever so beautiful. Idly, she wondered whether Charles and his men would be looking up into the same sky or whether they would be too busy trying to find order after last night's events. Snow had suffered so watching them scramble about, run in fear of the magical weather of Harlow's spell. It hadn't been enough to send her running away from Harlow herself, though. On the other hand, she was rather anticipating her presence. What a strange heart she had, that she still hoped that Harlow's truth was the tender care she had glimpsed on occasion and not the terrible anger she had witnessed last night. Charles' mother must have been right when she'd accused her of naiveté. A foolish girl, she'd called her. But then, she was sure that there was a way to Harlow's heart. Many had judged Harlow already – because she had magic and a temper, because she was shameless and sometimes so strange. Snow could afford to give her a chance, if only because Harlow had already done her worst and they had still ended up sharing a lover's embrace.

Dark orange had turned grayish blue by the time Harlow entered the room, which was now illuminated by the eerie glow of the moon and the fire crepitating in the hearth. The moon was half-full, betraying that their time together would have to come to an end and that Snow would have to make a decision that she had refused to think about so far. How could she, when she could hardly guess at Harlow's true intentions?

"Did you rest today?" Harlow asked upon first entering the room.

Snow nodded, looking at her under the pretty moonlight. She looked like a queen today, the square cleavage of her gown pushing her breasts up and putting them up for display, her corset tight and cinching her waist uncomfortably and her hair up and held together by a thin crown. Harlow didn't particularly favor such a headdress, so Snow mused that she must be trying to prove a point. Then, she wondered if she was the recipient of such display and why Harlow would think that she preferred this Evil Queen act over her softer manner.

Harlow kept herself at a distance, and after staring at Snow for a quiet moment, she looked away and crossed her arms over her chest. A displeased little gesture twisted her mouth.

"I sent a message to your husband," she said. "I proposed that we rekindle our truce and let bygones be bygones."

"Harlow, that's wond–"

"Even when it was he who broke our pact, and when he maimed two of my men in his heroic attempts to get to you."

Snow smiled, the curl of her lips soft, ever so soft, and something warm breaking inside her chest. "It was the right thing to do, the kind thing to do; to stop the bloodshed and let everyone see what I–"

"Enough!" Harlow turned to her again, a finger poised in the air as if she were scolding an annoying child. "I will say no more on the subject, and neither will you."

Harlow visibly relaxed after those words, her shoulders dropping and her posture opening up yet again. She looked sensual and powerful now, as if relaying the message of what she must have thought of as a concession to her enemy had left her feeling in command. Snow liked her either way, and loved her for controlling her worst instincts. Maybe she wasn't so foolish or naïve, maybe there was peace to be found in believing the best in someone.

"Come here now," Harlow said, offering her hand as she had done so many other nights, promises shining bright behind her eyes.

Snow followed her command, walking towards her and finding her after seven short steps. She counted each of them, finding focus in the mindless thought and hoping not to melt at Harlow's first touch. Their hands met shortly and, before Snow could enjoy the feeling, Harlow forced her to spin around and pressed herself to her back, keeping her still. Snow found herself staring at the tall mirror, the one Harlow had covered up with a blanket last night and which remained obscured by it.

"You don't like my mirrors," Harlow whispered against her ear, "and I figured I might try to change your mind."

"I don't–I don't think I understand."

Harlow moved back and Snow swayed on the spot, unbalanced. Harlow laughed and the sound moved with her, just a little terrifying as she walked around Snow in slow steps, reaching the mirror and removing the blanket in one sharp tug.

"Don't look at me, look at the lovely image you make in my looking glass."

Snow did as she was told, compelled to follow Harlow's demands by the deep sound of her beautiful voice and by her own desire, already pooling warm low in her belly.

Humming, Harlow mused, "I can't decide if I want to take that robe away myself, or have you do it."

"You do it," Snow requested thoughtlessly, biting her lip when Harlow raised a single eyebrow.

Harlow seemed amused by her nervousness, the smile that curved her lips next filling her eyes with mirth. She looked powerful as she walked back to Snow, and Snow didn't think it was a coincidence, or devoid of meaning.

Harlow pressed herself against Snow's back once again, and this time Snow couldn't ignore the picture that they painted in the mirror – Harlow's deft hands undoing the knot at the front of the robe and letting it fall open so that a strip of skin was revealed.

Harlow took her time with her, using her fingers to paint a path from Snow's collarbones and all the way down to the bushy hairs covering her pussy. She was soft, her fingers delicate as they went up and down a few times, lighting up Snow's skin. They rested between her breasts for a time, insinuating themselves over the swell of her chest, teasing more than touching.

Snow whined when Harlow pressed a barely-there kiss to her neck, and only then did Harlow stop her teasing. Harlow slid the robe down her shoulders, guiding her hands over Snow's arms so that it fell away from her and pooled at her feet. Cold hit Snow's skin, but what made her move her arms up was embarrassment, her instinct to cover herself up.

"None of that, now," Harlow ordered, grasping her wrists and pulling her arms down. She forced them to the small of her back so that Snow had to arch her shoulders, her breasts jiggling forward at their small struggle.

Harlow kissed the back of her neck and then bent down for a moment. She came back up with the sash that had held the robe together between her hands. Then, she tied it up neatly about Snow's wrists, leaving her hands firmly clasped behind her and her body on display for the mirror before them.

Harlow left one more kiss on the back of Snow's shoulder and cooed, "Come on now, take a nice, long look. You are the most beautiful woman in the world, don't deny yourself the pleasure."

Snow laughed, nervous and incensed, and slightly uncomfortable as well. "That's silly," she murmured. "You're far more b–"

"Hush, I said."

Harlow's arms came about her once more, and her thumb touched the underside of her right breast lovingly. Snow watched a smile spread across Harlow's lips, satisfied and predatory, and it was only then that she dared really look at the picture she painted in the mirror. The skin Harlow's thumb was touching was purple, made so by an insistent kiss she'd pressed there not two nights ago. Snow had keened at the attention and had panted her way to the heights of pleasure with only a gentle tug on her clit. She blushed now thinking about it, and she watched the color paint her cheeks and her chest, her pale skin made vibrant by the reddish tint.

There was another bruise at the base of her neck, and Harlow's mouth was already making sure that it didn't fade, her lips sucking carefully around the skin so that the touch was almost painful, but mostly delightful. Harlow licked at it, too, and Snow felt herself shake inside her embrace, grateful that she was being held.

Harlow's lips traveled up her neck. She bit at her ear and murmured, "You're not really looking, Snow. I want you to look at how pretty you are when I touch you."

Snow closed her eyes at the insistence, shy before a mirror that she knew would show her naked and wanting while in the arms of a woman in control, dressed and composed like a queen. She didn't want to see the need written inside her own eyes or the distance that she guessed would be clouding Harlow's. Harlow uttered her disapproval and once again dropped her arms away from Snow, and walked away. Snow keened at the loss, opening her eyes and pulling at the restraints about her hands, now suddenly feeling trapped and rooted to the spot.

Harlow didn't go far, instead prowling before her like a beast happy to tease her prey. Snow watched her pace, but then brought her eyes to the mirror. Naked, hands tied at her back, she was fully exposed. She felt strange at appraising herself, yet she did, watching the slope of her hips, how they were slightly disproportionate to her thin waist. Her thighs, thick and strong, the right one scarred deeply above her knee from a fall she'd taken in the battlefield at the beginning of the war. Charles had been terribly upset when her skin had been marred so; Harlow, upon first discovering it, had licked at its edges carefully, only moving upwards and to the apex of Snow's thighs when Snow had begged her for it.

Arousal was obvious when Snow looked at herself, sweat pooling low on her brow and red flush still painting her face, her neck and her chest. Her breathing was rapid and her breasts bounced lightly with it, her pink nipples made darker with lust and pebbled now that she didn't have her robe and Harlow remained stubbornly away.

"I don't–" she started, interrupting herself because she wasn't sure what it was she wanted to say. She licked her lips to take a moment and continued, "I don't see that it is such an enticing picture when you're not in it."

"Let's see if we can fix that, then. Kneel for me."

Snow faced Harlow's defiant eyes, pulling at her restrains and feeling the soft sash about them pull back and keep her in place. Awkwardly, with her shoulders stretched and her hands useless, she went to her knees, sitting back on her haunches and looking up at Harlow, now made queen not by her headdress, but by Snow's easy subjugation. Harlow's smile was bitter and Snow felt suddenly out of her depth, devoid of any understanding she'd ever hoped to have of the woman before her.

"Now that looks like somet–"

"Why are you being cruel?" Snow interrupted.

"Cruel, you say? Oh no, darling princess. Cruel would have been to keep you in the dungeons, to torture you and feed you nothing but water and hard bread. Cruel would have been to rip your husband's heart the moment he stepped into my kingdom."

"But I–"

"You promised your service, Snow! That was our deal, and instead you question me before my advisors, you make me yield before my enemies, you–"

"You did what you believed was right! You didn't bow to Charles because I asked but because you knew there was nothing to gain in shedding more blood," Snow countered, passionate, standing up as much as her knees allowed her and unwittingly reaching for Harlow, wishing she wasn't still that tall, powerful creature before her. "You are not evil, Harlow, and you would do well to not believe your own legend."

Harlow laughed and turned away from her for a small moment, only to finally stalk back to Snow once she seemed to have recovered herself. She kneeled behind Snow and surrounded her with strong arms. Snow toppled backwards and into the embrace, surprised by the sudden display. Harlow kept up her rough handling, curling one hand inside Snow's hair and pulling, forcing her neck back. Snow grunted but had no time to complain when Harlow's other hand delved between her thighs. Harlow pushed two fingers inside her and kept them there, curling the tips slowly so that Snow's insides burned around them.

"How do you refuse to see the worst in me? You of all people?" Harlow whispered, baring her teeth.

Parting her lips, Snow forbid herself from speaking her truth. *I love you,* she would confess. *Let me in, please, let me into your heart,* she would beg. She didn't want to break herself open and let Harlow see all her vulnerabilities.

In any case, Snow could hardly think when she was looking at Harlow's fingers pushing in and out of her now, her pussy lips swollen and made dark pink before her very eyes, the mirror betraying her most intimate secrets.

Harlow laughed against her neck, biting at the purple bruise there and giving another soft pull to her hair, forcing Snow to elongate her body and expose it to the looking glass. Snow could only look at Harlow's hand between her legs, though, now parted wantonly to allow her movement, her hips trying to follow the staccato rhythm of Harlow's fingers.

"I think you would do anything for me, Snow White, wouldn't you?" Harlow hummed her question, her words barely intelligible as she bit at Snow's shoulder and soothed the skin with her pretty, pink tongue, only to bite again.

Harlow looked playful and vicious both now, beautiful in that strange way of hers that made it seem as if she was miles away, rather than cradling Snow's body and diverting herself with it. Snow stayed quiet, moaning instead at the onslaught of sensation conquering her body, refusing to declare her feelings and have Harlow trample over them.

"Look at you, after all," Harlow continued, hiding herself from Snow now to travel the expanse of her back with her lips, pressing them to the back of her neck and causing warm shivers to run down her skin and pool at her pussy, between her folds, at the core of her pleasure.

Harlow whispered, "You were so wet even as we were fighting. My fingers slid right in, and I think you're asking for more. Do you want a third, darling? Would you ask nicely?"

Snow did, and parting her legs as far as they would go, she asked, "Yes, please, please one more."

Harlow didn't make her wait, pushing a third finger up inside her and curling them all at her knuckles, already knowing how much Snow liked that, how it was usually a preamble to the peak of her pleasure. Snow moaned, curling herself forward so as to better accommodate herself, ignoring her burning shoulders and the tight pull at her wrists in favor of the slick pleasure between her legs. Harlow played with her thumb until she could expose Snow's clit to the mirror, and Snow looked at the small nub, dark purple in its desire, and parted her lips in a careful sigh at the sight of Harlow touching her. Harlow circled the skin slowly, even when her fingers were insistent and fast inside her now.

"What else? What else do you need?"

"My breasts, I, if you touch–"

Harlow removed her hand from Snow's hair, letting her head drop forward and her neck rest. She brought Snow closer as she embraced her and cupped her left breast, squeezing it tenderly between her fingers and running them about its contour, taking her time to caress about her nipple with her fingertips, thumbing at it only once it was fully hard.

"And a kiss," Snow requested. "Kiss me."

"Not that. You don't deserve kisses today."

Harlow punctuated her denial with a sharp tug to her nipple. Snow whined, at the harsh treatment, at being rejected, but also at Harlow's fingers inside her, now curling themselves in and out of her with purpose. Snow gave into it, searching for Harlow's touch with her hips and hurting her knees against the floor as she ground herself harder. Harlow grabbed at her other breast and cupped it fully. There was a small roughness to her palm, right at the base of her fingers, and the feel of it against her nipple made Snow shudder, fall forward as she felt heat seizing her very insides. Her walls trembled around Harlow's fingers, and with Harlow's thumb playing so very carefully with her clit, Snow gave into the cresting bliss that took her over.

She was exhausted, and her moan was both pleasure and relief, loud as it had never been before. Harlow's rapid, hot breathing behind her made her open her eyes wide and lean backwards, looking for her touch, silently begging her to not move away.

"Easy, princess, I'm not done with you yet."

Harlow pushed her forward and Snow toppled over without putting up any resistance. Her face and chest met the cold stone floor and she lost sight of the mirror, of herself and Harlow both. She felt suddenly lost, her connection with Harlow, already feeble, now completely gone. She noticed how pasty her mouth felt, and how her shoulders, already burning from the pull of the ties, were stretched tighter by the position, her back arched as her hips and ass remained high up in the air, her knees firmly planted against the floor. She breathed out harshly, feeling hot and cold at the same time, her hard nipples uncomfortable where they touched the floor and her insides still burning, her thighs warm from her own juices.

Harlow showed her no mercy, pressing her mouth to her oversensitive folds and kissing with care but relentlessly, using her tongue to play. With every lick, every small touch, Snow felt herself sweating, felt her legs grow weaker, shakier, her blood leave her face and chest and pool between her legs, where new pleasure was building even when the old one hadn't quite left, so that every touch was bliss and torture both. She kept on hearing

Harlow's pants as well, her harsh breathing that made her touches clumsier than usual. She felt the pressure of Harlow's fingers on her hips and her ass, her nails digging in at times so that Snow knew Harlow was trembling. They were moving together towards ecstasy, yet Harlow remained a mystery, behind her, controlling, refusing to be touched.

Snow's body climbed towards pleasure once more, yet Harlow refused to liberate her, keeping her in place and pushing her soft mouth to the flesh of her ass, the back of her trembling thighs, her tied wrists and her restless fingers, her burning shoulders and the expanse of her back, down her spine and back up again, lingering at her neck and biting carefully. Harlow was worshipping her, but she wouldn't look at her and she wouldn't stop, and Snow felt something heavy fill her stomach, a lead-like guilt pulsing inside her because she wanted more, she wanted this but so much more. Harlow's adoration wasn't enough; it was the shadow of what Snow needed from her. Harlow refused to be something other than the powerful queen at her back, and so her devotion felt like a game, a terrible, terrible game.

"Stop, please," Snow begged after a long time, "please, stop."

Harlow did, and Snow felt her draw away, her absence immediately sinking her into despair. She pulled at the ties around her wrists, fighting them with true intention this time, wanting them gone. She was desperate. She was in pain – her knees, her shoulders, her wrists. She was weary to the bone, so she cried out when Harlow untied the sash and helped her turn around and sit down on the floor. She said nothing, watching as Harlow moved in a flurry of fabric and clumsy limbs to put a robe around her shoulders. Snow looked at her only once she'd stopped and she saw her pale, ill-looking, her eyes red and her mouth like a bruise, her hands trembling.

"I should leave," Harlow whispered, her voice small and inadequate.

Snow didn't stop her, didn't know how to or whether she wanted to, and Harlow left. Once alone, Snow hugged her knees to her chest and cried soft, quiet tears.

The days that followed were confusing. Harlow avoided Snow and Snow avoided Harlow in return, and as the days passed, Snow watched the moon grow larger each night, counting down to the end of their unusual truce. Snow was meant to make a choice soon, and now that her time and thoughts weren't constantly filled by Harlow, she tried to think about it coldly. If she was to be sensible, then surely she should choose to return to her husband, to decide on the path that would cast out this would-be Evil Queen and put the kingdom in her hands and those of her fair prince. Choose her husband, who had saved her; deny her lover, who had once upon a time tried to kill her. It shouldn't be such a hard decision to make.

Snow spent her days wandering the palace, lost, and resting in her mother's old room, looking at the skies and thinking about how much she loved this view and how terribly she had missed it. She felt groundless, much like she had after the days of her mother's death, when she'd had no purpose.

Growing up, she had been a strange child. Neglected by the king, she had had no education but her mother's storybooks, no passion but the forests surrounding the palace, and no rules but to remain unobtrusive. Sometimes, the king would catch sight of her and would look at her for a long moment as if he couldn't place her, as if it wasn't his blood running through her veins. Mother would often say that her destiny would have been different had she been a boy, but Snow had always doubted it. The king had thought himself eternal, and so he'd always refused words that suggested he choose an heir, or at the very least a proper husband for his daughter.

The king had been a cruel man, prone to harsh judgment and devoid of mercy. He'd been a man of blood and battle, and Snow had known him to be barbarous even to those close to him. Her mother had feared him, so Snow had learnt to be wary of him and to keep out of his way.

After her mother had died, Snow had drifted. She had floated about her palace life, roaming the kitchens as much as she had the beautiful halls, and most of all walking about the forests, shoeless and wild. It had been a purposeless and lonely existence. She had shied away from other noble girls the most, envious of their grace and their education. They had thought her strange, too, and she'd fancied that they'd envied her freedom to run around wildly while they were stuck inside with their tutors and governesses. They couldn't know that Snow would have loved to sit down for a lesson on the knowledge they took for granted. Snow had always been intuitive, and her mother's love for books and stories had kept her sharp, but she'd envied those girls the ability to pinpoint their castle on a map and to name their parents' commercial trade, as well as their refined manners. She'd had her birds and her trees and her books, but as she fleeted alone around them, with no companion and no family, she had felt herself become an illusion.

Harlow's arrival had changed that. Suddenly, the king was no longer and in his stead, a strange creature remained. Snow had felt glad at the king's demise, and guilty too at such a thought, which was vindictive in a way she didn't know she could be. He'd made her mother so very miserable, though, and this new queen had looked so sad as well.

Harlow's own oddities had been a balm to Snow's loneliness. She had sought her out relentlessly from that first moment when she'd grabbed her hand, and Harlow had taken to her quietly, accepting her presence if remaining tight-lipped about her feelings. They had never talked a great deal, but they had shared quiet evenings in the palace's studies, Harlow pouring over books and teaching herself the matters of the kingdom. She had made the king's advisors into her tutors, and hadn't minded Snow's presence during their meetings.

Sometimes, they would speak of the forests outside and Harlow's eyes would turn soft, yearning, so that Snow would see the nymph that she was underneath her queenly clothes. Harlow's queerness had kept everyone at bay, but it had grounded Snow. Harlow had brought the spirit of the forest with her and she had given Snow an unwitting gift – the raspy edges at the end of her laughter, and the soft pressure of their thighs touching during the winter solstice fires. They had understood each other in silences and with intuition, and Snow had thought she'd found a place by Harlow's side, had believed herself privy to her mysteries. She had craved her friendship and perhaps she had desired her as well, if she'd been unable to understand such feelings when younger and inexperienced.

She hadn't known Harlow as well as she'd thought, or perhaps she had been too naïve to believe that there was danger in her spell. Even during the last years, when Harlow had started spending long hours inside her mirror room, alone in the darkness and chased by shadows, Snow had remained unwilling to believe her a threat. And the truth of the matter was, after everything, even today she was convinced that Harlow's darkness wasn't shallow and that it came from deep despair.

Three days passed and still Harlow refused to seek her out. Harlow had her queenly duties to entertain herself while Snow spent her days wandering around, trying to find her center.

Snow had taken to pestering the kitchen staff to avoid the dining hall, and to striking up conversations with noblemen around the palace, asking them questions about Harlow without thinking of the need for subtlety. She wanted to know what it was that people saw when they looked at their queen and why they believed rebellion had arisen in the past. After all, Snow had given the kingdom no reason to want her for a ruler, and Harlow's hand hadn't been cruel.

"Honestly, Your Highness," Mrs. Agnes told her after Snow had annoyed her enough with her questions. "She's a witch, and so shameless about it, too."

"You would turn your back on her?"

"No one in this palace would, but many outside of it would happily burn her at the stake. Better a feeble-minded princess than a sorceress, they'll say. Surely she drinks blood to keep her beauty, they'll say."

"A feeble-minded princess?"

Mrs. Agnes scoffed, amused as she indulged Snow's curiosity. "Running around with no shoes, Your Highness, and with your mother such a sickly creature, of course the world thinks you a little loose in the head. If you don't mind me saying so."

Snow pursed her lips, thinking of how unfair rumors could be, of how the power of legend could make them out to be creatures of myth, rather than simple people with simple tastes.

However so, her line of questions brought much the same answer from servants and noblemen alike, if no one was quite as open as Mrs. Agnes had been. Many suggested that Harlow's crime against her had been what had convinced the people of the queen's evilness, and that seeing Snow return to fight for her place and in the arms of a handsome prince had been enough to condemn the queen altogether.

"Perhaps it is fair that the crown belongs to you and your prince, Your Highness," one of the youngest ladies of the court told her. "Don't you miss him terribly? To be imprisoned here so, I couldn't imagine."

As many had before, the girl looked at Snow's wrists as she spoke. They still wore the marks of Harlow's ties, a soft reddening about them and a greenish bruise on the inside of her right wrist. Snow didn't mind them. She liked them, in fact, and she often found herself touching them softly as she stared into the distance. The bruise was were Harlow most liked to touch her and it made her think of their dinners together, of laughing quietly, and of Harlow flirting with coyness and placing her hands casually on Snow's hand, her palm, her wrist, sometimes her elbow. Sometimes such tender touches were enough to make Snow squirm, to awaken her body to the promise of pleasure. Now, that small point of pain was enough to remind her of Harlow's touch and to make her yearn for it.

She didn't miss her husband, was the truth. Thoughts of him were fleeting and uncomfortable, the loyalty she held towards him making her feel guilty. Charles had saved her, he had given her a home, he had started a war in her name. He was her champion and he was meant to be her companion. But she didn't miss him.

Harlow was a different matter entirely, for Snow had missed her even when she'd known better than to hope for a reconciliation. She missed her now, too, for even as she did her best to avoid her, she unwittingly sought her out. She kept speaking about her to anyone who would listen, even to the unresponsive wind as she waded her way through the forests. She talked about her to the singing birds, and wished for them to answer.

On the third day of her estrangement, Snow's quiet contemplations of the morning sky were interrupted by Harlow's chambermaid, the shy-looking girl she had spoken to not long ago.

After an awkward curtsy, the girl said, "Her Majesty bids me give you this."

She offered up a sealed parchment and Snow took it with curiosity. She turned it about in her hands and immediately noticed Charles' seal emblazoned in the red wax holding it closed.

"And she didn't read it?" she questioned, more to herself than to the girl and expecting no answer.

"Her advisors expressed their worry, Your Highness, but Her Majesty did not. She–I–well, she *demands,* oh, do pardon my saying so, but the queen, she–"

"Yes, what is her demand?"

"She demands you read the missive and answer in kind. She would have me express her trust in your judgment regarding your deal and this war."

Snow threw her hands up at those words, frustrated even as contentment pressed on her chest. What a baffling woman Harlow could be.

"She might have come up and said this herself," Snow complained. "But to give up her pride, to forbid herself from stubbornness once, no, of course she wouldn't."

"Your Highness, I…"

Snow apologized to the girl quickly, mindful of her flushed cheeks and her awkward demeanor. Harlow shouldn't have put her in the situation of delivering such a message in the first place, but Snow shouldn't make her witness of her temper, either. She sent her away.

The missive still in her hands, Snow sat down by her window, where the light was brighter. She broke the seal and opened the letter, which was indeed written in Charles' even calligraphy and held his signature. He wrote of his choice to wade into Harlow's kingdom and of the terrible storm that had stopped his advance. He wrote of Harlow's agreement to reinstate the truce and how he thought it a retreat and a sure sign that she had given up, and couldn't hope to win this war. He wrote that he would do as Snow bid, that he would brave Harlow's ire once again to get to her and to rescue her from sure torture. He wrote of battle and honor, of vengeance, blood, of conquering the darkness that had been devouring this kingdom since the Evil Queen had lawlessly lain her claim upon it. His last words were *my princess, my magical princess, were I to receive no answer later than four days from now, I shall believe you in grave danger and fight my way to you, and to your crown.*

"My crown?" she murmured, hugging herself as her mind raced with the words before her. She closed her eyes, something heavy settling inside her stomach. "Oh Charles, sweet Charles, how unfair I have been to you. How untrue and senseless."

For she didn't love him, and she didn't want him to rescue her again. Yet she had married him and had claimed a place by his side. She had allowed him this war, the hope for this crown that she had never wanted herself, and she would break his heart. She would, she was sure, for even if she denied Harlow in the end, she couldn't possibly stay with him, not when her heart so foolishly longed for another.

Snow disentangled herself from her position, sniffing as she did so, fighting the tears that were pooling at the corners of her eyes. She no longer knew why she wanted to cry, and she no longer wished to play Harlow's game. She would write back to Charles and then she would confront Harlow. She would decide upon her future then, and would disentangle Harlow's intentions. She had loved Harlow's mysteries long enough, and now she would have to choose whether or not to love her truths.

Her letter was hasty but thoughtful, and she wrote it hoping that Charles would respect her request to stop any action against Harlow. She told him the truth – that she had been given free reign of the palace, and that no harm had come to her.

She climbed down from her tower in search of Harlow once she was done, the missive folded between her trembling fingers. She wasn't sure what she would say to convince Harlow to share her secrets, but she would beg if necessary. Pride had never been her sin, and if Harlow's own forced her to keep herself hidden, then Snow would fight her by discovering herself.

She came upon one of Harlow's advisors standing by the mirror room, and she feared the queen to be locked inside it. The door was half-open so Snow peeked inside the room, trying to see something within the shadows. She blinked when she saw a figure moving about, and sure that she had found Harlow, she entered it, not heeding the advisor's exclamation to keep away. As soon as she was inside, the doors closed behind her, secret power banging them together and surprising her with both the booming sound and the sudden loss of light. She brought both hands to her chest as she turned to look at the now closed doors.

"What happened? What–Harlow? Harlow, are you here?"

She heard laughter, but it wasn't Harlow's, and Snow was sure it didn't belong to this world. It came from all around her as if carried by the wind, as if its owner was flying about her, unseen, fading in an out, impossibly close one moment and the next far away, almost gone.

"It's just tricks of the mind, Snow, don't be silly."

However, even as she spoke, she heard whispers here and there, growing closer as she stood still by the doors. She turned towards the inside of the room again, her eyes half-closed to adjust to the darkness. The curtains were drawn, that was all. There was nothing to fear. Repeating such words, Snow took a step forward, intent on reaching the drapes and letting more light into the room. Now, with barely a few sunrays filtering through the heavy fabrics, the shadows played tricks with the mirrors, making it seem as if invisible creatures were moving about, jumping from place to place.

Snow's steps were loud, or at least they felt so to her. She walked slowly, minding her way, forcing her eyes to not stray and look about at the dozens of looking glasses trying to make a fool out of her. The further she walked, the colder she felt, and soon she was bringing her arms about herself, a frosty and strange touch cooling her skin where it wasn't protected around her neck and on her face. Her hands too grew stiff, and she closed and opened them a couple of times to get them to loosen up. Her fingers refused her even when she shook them, shaping her hands into rigid claws and rendering them insensitive.

A shadow crossed her path and Snow stopped walking. Then, there was a whisper. And then, many more. She looked about herself, seeing nothing and seeing too much at the same time, sudden panic gripping her and confusing her senses. She wasn't alone here, yet she must be, for Harlow's whispers were hers and hers alone. She could hear them now, though, upsetting as they grew louder, as they became a continuous hum that banged against her ears.

"What are you?" she mumbled, and the laughter came back, wrapping itself about the noise that seemed like voices but maybe wasn't there at all.

Snow turned around once, twice, searching for the truth and finding only shades of grey, puzzling pictures that weren't really there, glimpses of light traveling between mirrors so that Snow could see herself in the shadows as well, a lonely figure searching for the invisible. The atmosphere grew heavier, colder, and Snow felt as if unseen hands were pressing down on her, around her shoulders and trying to bring her down. She shook violently, trying to rid herself of the ghostly touch. The feeling didn't go away and instead it turned viscous, like she imagined snakes would feel slithering up her spine. Her mouth parted on an uncomfortable groan. The whispers grew louder still, creeping up around her and making the shadows tangible, turning them into monsters.

Snow walked forward, searching for the light and fighting to remember herself. The spell around her made her movements sluggish so that the drapes looked miles and miles away, reflections in the mirrors making the spaces longer and narrower. Snow told herself it was a silly vision, yet when she caught sight of color out of the corner of her eye, she followed it unwittingly. It escaped from her and Snow's limbs unlocked, allowed her to run after it, making her way through the obscurity of the room until she no longer knew where she stood, where the door had been, where the windows rested. The chamber proved deeper than a forest, but Snow followed the image nonetheless, watched it move from mirror to mirror and take shape before her eyes so that soon she realized the color she'd been following was that of Harlow's hair.

"Harlow!" she screamed, loud so that her voice would rise above the pervasive whispers of whatever spell was being cast inside this room.

There was no answer. Snow yelled Harlow's name again and kept running. Over and over she did the same, thinking that she must be running in circles, or that she was journeying past the veil of the mortal world.

"Harlow!" she yelled once more when she felt she was close to the figure that kept evading her.

Abruptly, she crashed into something face first. The impact threw her back and the sudden pain on her face and arms helped sharpen her focus. She whined softly as she touched her own nose and her forehead. They felt tender, as did her elbows and arms. As she felt for bruises, she took a step back and realized that she had bodily crashed into a wide standing mirror. She looked into its surface and didn't see herself but Harlow, her figure a trick played by magic reflections. Snow moved closer, brought her hand up as if to touch the looking glass, but didn't get there. Instead, her hand remained poised in the air, a breath away from the fuzzy image reflecting back at her.

The Harlow from behind the glass stood before an obscure background, and Snow found herself unconsciously searching for her eyes and wishing to see the light inside them. Harlow was looking down, however, at a red apple between her hands. The color of the fruit stood over everything else so that Snow almost believed it to be real. It looked ripe, fresh, the rouge skin covered in dew and asking to be bitten. The apple would be crisp, Snow knew, and it would taste sweet. It would be the most delicious apple in the world, and Snow knew because she had tasted it.

"Why would you show me this?" Snow wondered. Laughter was her answer, the otherworldly sound of the creatures from beyond, of whatever enchantment lived behind these mirrors.

Sound fluttered around her still, like that of hundreds of butterflies taking flight around her. Snow thought she heard words, but she couldn't make a clear speech in the confusing murmurs. She ignored them in favor of staring at the picture before her, at the figure of Harlow that had been preserved for her behind the looking glass, her long hair obscuring her face and her eyes downcast and staring at an apple, maybe pondering her decision, or maybe regretting the choice she had already made. Either way, Snow had bitten the apple.

"Why would you show me this?" she repeated, thinking it callous cruelty, a sure sign that she wasn't wanted here.

There was no answer this time, and just as Snow was about to ask her question again, light flooded the chamber. She turned her head towards the sudden sunlight and closed her eyes briefly, trying to adjust now that the shadows were gone. She saw someone opening the drapes and now sure that there were no visions left, she took comfort when she recognized Harlow's fiery hair and graceful movements.

"What are you doing here?" Harlow asked without looking at her, still busy with the many windows of the room, and seemingly intending to part every set of curtains.

Snow couldn't tell whether Harlow was angry or not, but she was glad of her presence either way. Giving no answer, she looked once again at the mirror before her, and saw only her reflection staring back at her. She was pale as a ghost. She looked about herself and realized that she was in the middle of the room, not far away from the double set of doors, or even from the window that she had been trying to reach before starting to run. Where had she run to, exactly, if not further inside the room? There must have indeed been spell inside the chamber, wishing to trick her.

"Snow, darling Snow, what are you doing here? Are you harmed? Are you–"

Harlow was by her in an instant, bringing her cool hands up to her face, cupping her cheeks and then touching her shoulders, her arms, moving her hands from place to place as if to make sure that Snow was there and that she was well. Snow soaked up the attention, suddenly aware of how much she'd longed for Harlow's touch, how much their separation had weighted on her. Harlow kissed her forehead and her cheek, still manic.

"You feel feverish, you must be sick."

"I'm only tired," Snow said after a moment, her voice raw, as if she'd been yelling. "I ran, Harlow, I ran for so long and I am only in the middle of the room. These mirrors play tricks on the mind, do they not? What lives behind them? What mocked me so?"

Harlow moved back, keeping her hands on Snow's cheeks but stopping her sweet kisses. She searched for her eyes and Snow stared back openly, yearning for answers and tired of Harlow's games.

"You heard them?" Harlow asked, and her voice too was hoarse, full of unshed tears.

"What did I hear?"

"The fae, darling, the fairy folk teasing you, only teasing. But no one has heard them before," Harlow said, thoughtful even as her eyes didn't leave Snow's. "Everyone thinks me a mad woman, talking to the shadows."

Snow's mouth twisted sideways, shades of a smile shaping her lips. "I fail to see how speaking to the fae would be better in the eyes of the court."

Harlow laughed, the sound deep and rich, the edges raspy and sensual. Harlow should always laugh, Snow thought, and laughed herself.

Harlow brought her close, putting her arms around her waist her and molding their bodies together, filling Snow's empty spaces with her limbs and the sweet smell of her skin. Snow brought her arms around her as well, and clung to the back of her dress with her stiff fingers.

"I have missed you," Harlow confessed, low against her ear. A gust of wind blew at the same time and Snow wondered whether it was the wind at all, or the fairy folk angered by the tenderness hidden in Harlow's voice.

"You have been avoiding me."

"So have you."

Snow nodded, the gesture imperceptible as she pressed her face to the hollow of Harlow's neck, seeking her warmth. If only they could stay like this forever and never let go. If only there wasn't a world outside hanging in the balance of their affair.

"Harlow, you must tell me what it is we are doing," Snow requested finally. "Had you thrown me in the dungeons, or fashioned me into a maid, or–or cut my head upon my arrival, I believe I would understand you better."

"That's foolish, darling. You would make a terrible maid."

Snow laughed despite herself, and loved that Harlow was laughing too. She wondered that they could have this easy warmth between them when their past suggested battle and blood, when just three days ago Harlow had refused to look at her when she'd so desperately needed her to.

"I do mean my words," Snow insisted, hoping to come across as half-way serious even when her speech still bubbled with the remnants of laughter.

Harlow pressed a small, wet kiss against her throat and for a moment, Snow feared she would be distracted from her purposes once more. However, Harlow broke their embrace and took her hand, leading her out of the mirror room. Snow followed without hesitation, wanting to be with Harlow as much as she wanted to leave the chamber and its mysteries behind.

Snow stopped their movement briefly, remembering why she had been looking for Harlow in the first place. She gave her the letter that she had crumpled between her hands. Harlow listened with half an ear and dropped the missive with one of her advisors, dismissive of the fact that whichever words Snow had written could lead to an all-out war once more. They might even if Snow had been genuine, for Charles could interpret her plea as the forced acquiescence of a prisoner of war. Apparently uncaring of such matters, Harlow kept on leading her forward and only stopped once she had reached the double set of stairs that climbed to both towers of the palace. Upon sensing her doubt, Snow made the decision for them and pulled them up the northern tower so that they could talk in her mother's old room, rather than in Harlow's own. She had had enough of mirrors to last her a lifetime.

Harlow followed without offering resistance, but halfway up the long staircase, she said, "I have never been up here."

"I did wonder that you didn't change it at all."

"It seemed disrespectful that I should."

Snow hummed as they climbed, pondering Harlow's words. There had been two twin towers, similar dwellings on opposite sides of the palace, and Harlow had made one her abode and had never stepped on the second one.

They entered the chambers and Snow put distance between them immediately, sitting by the windowsill and leaving Harlow to stand in the middle of the room. She was still shaken, and she couldn't trust herself to not beg for Harlow's embrace and ignore her own wishes for explanations. Her hands were still stiff and she felt cold, so she grabbed a coverlet and set it around her shoulders. Harlow looked about and finally sat down at the edge of Snow's bed timidly, as if trying to occupy as little space as possible. She seemed stiff herself, not quite as natural as she usually was, so Snow stayed quiet and willed her to speak, instead of prodding for quick answers.

A little time passed as they breathed together. Snow was glad for the reprieve, which allowed her to shake her hands awake and calm her pounding heart down.

Eventually, Harlow spoke, "My mother too lived in this palace, did you know?"

"I–"

"No, of course you did not. Even if you heard the rumors no one knew she was my mother; no one knew what happened to her, no one cared."

Harlow wasn't looking at her. Instead, she was looking past her, at the clear sky outside or maybe at a blank point on the wall. Snow couldn't decide whether she sounded angry or weary, and only knew that she had never heard that quality on Harlow's voice. Something yearning, perhaps, or lost.

"She lived in the tower, my tower," she continued, telling her story and pretending detachment even if her whole demeanor was awkward. "So did my aunt. They were twins, and they were both so beautiful, so unfairly alluri–"

"The women from the painting," Snow interrupted.

"Yes," Harlow replied, an imperceptible shift to the direction of her gaze putting her eyes before Snow's, so that they were now looking at each other.

Keeping their eyes locked together, Harlow spun a tale for her in clipped words and an even tone, compelling Snow to not interrupt by never giving herself a chance to pause. However, Snow couldn't deny the anguish behind Harlow's act of disinterest, and as her voice shaped a story of deep tragedy, Snow began to understand. Not wholly, for how could she? But as Harlow weaved her words with efficiency and without flourishes, she saw before her the child that she had been, born in beauty and peace, and yet brought up for revenge not her own, for anger that shouldn't have been hers to command. How cruel Harlow's mother had been, settling her own pain on her daughter's shoulders and making her responsible of avenging it. And yet, how Snow wished her own mother had had some of that same barbarous impetuousness, so that Snow may have grown brave enough to defy the king's savagery.

"My mother died," Harlow said, giving her story a tragic corollary.

Even when speaking such words, Harlow remained stoic and stiff, playing her game of shadows and denying herself sadness. Snow said nothing, letting the pause in Harlow's story linger between them. She could taste the tension, and hoped to take her cue from Harlow. Whether she wanted comfort or was looking for confrontation Snow didn't know, yet she found herself hard-pressed to provide either. Nothing in Harlow's story explained the darkness that had crawled its way between them, after all, nothing clarified how Harlow's murder of the king translated to her intentions of doing away with Snow. And above all, nothing hinted at the reasons behind their current affair.

Harlow broke her gaze away from Snow's and looked down at her own hands, now hovering above her stomach as if refusing to fully settle down there. She now looked confused, and Snow wondered if she had ever shared this tale before. She didn't think so. Harlow must have been leading a lonely life, lost in this court and kingdom that had never questioned her origins if not to condemn her for an evil sorceress. *If you'd only talked to me,* Snow thought. But then, to think that Harlow would easily confess to the crime of killing the king to his daughter was foolish.

Harlow closed her fist suddenly, and the movement held such strain that Snow felt it physically, and her shoulders jumped in surprise. Harlow pounded her fist against her own stomach hard enough that Snow worried she would hurt herself, and so jumped forward a step, intending to reach out and stop her. Harlow stopped without Snow's intrusion, even if she still held her fist closed tight and pressed to the space between her chest and stomach.

"I had this weight inside my stomach. It kept growing and growing and gro–" She interrupted herself, seemingly choked up. She swallowed the emotion back up, blinking her eyes fast as if to fight tears.

"Harlow, I–"

"It felt like a stone," she said, looking up again and searching for Snow's eyes.

She settled her gaze there, as if daring Snow to look away from her sudden anguish. Whether she expected Snow would turn away from such challenge or meet it head on Snow couldn't know. She knew, though, that she could never look away, not when Harlow was on the brink of confession and when her walls were falling apart even as her closed fist fought to keep them high and mighty.

Harlow swallowed noticeably again, and repeated, "It felt like a stone. Then–Then the king died, and so did Mother. As if her life was some price to pay, as if she hadn't paid enough already, and I… I felt so light, suddenly." She laughed awkwardly, and the bubbles of her laughter mixed themselves with her grief until they sounded like fresh tears. "And it was such a terrible feeling, to feel so light. I thought it would be liberating, and good, so good after a lifetime of the weight of revenge, but I only felt so, so, so very… I don't know, so–"

"Groundless?"

"Yes."

"Like you could just disappear and it wouldn't matter, because you were never real in the first place."

"That's… yes, I suppose. Purposeless, and lost."

"I was lost too, for a time," Snow confessed, breaking away from her awkward position and moving closer to Harlow, suddenly realizing that the few steps that separated them felt like an impossible distance to cover. "After my mother died, and until you came to the palace. I never feel lost when I'm with you."

Harlow reacted hardly to that, standing up and opening her fist. Her features turned abruptly fierce and she leaned forward, as if a beast ready to pounce.

"Don't say that! After what I have done, the pain I have caused you." Ferocity became heartache when Harlow spoke, her voice a weak thread that was barely loud enough for Snow to make out her words.

Snow denied her the pleasure of self-pity, and shrugged as she made her feelings clear and simple. "The thing is, Harlow, I love you."

"Don't!"

"Oh, I will if I want to," Snow stated, grabbing at the coverlet still around her shoulders and hugging herself with it as if in need of a shield. It was hard for her to be forceful, but she wouldn't let Harlow intimidate her into stopping her revelation.

"Are you going to stand there and tell me that you love me?" Harlow scorned, pride cutting through her anguish and pushing her into her most regal character. Mocking, as if even the thought of Snow's confessed feelings was ridiculous, she said, "If you had any sense you would hate me."

"I did hate you! I woke up and I hated you as I never had before; I was so angry; I felt so misplaced–"

"Good, y–"

"You took everything from me," Snow stated, moving forward and towards Harlow once more if shying away from crowding her space. Holding her gaze steady even when she could feel tears pushing at the corners of her eyes, she continued, "You pushed me away from my home, from the court and the servants that raised me, from these forests that I love and the only sky I have ever known. You forced me to run away, you forced me to understand real fear. And worst-worst of all, you showed me that you didn't care, that you wanted me gone."

She stopped and swallowed, her throat now feeling so tight that it was painful, that it hurt to push words past her lips. She held her stance, and let feelings that she had buried for years leave the tightly coiled place inside her heart.

"I was so angry, and with that anger I married Charles, and I believed him when he spoke of revenge so I thought I wanted it, too. I was angry enough that war felt like the only answer, because I hated you, Harlow, I hated you for throwing away the years we spent together as if they were nothing."

"Where is all that hatred now, then, darling? Why haven't you run a knife into my chest yet? No one would blame you for it."

Snow threw her arms up, letting go of the coverlet and letting her body breath with incredulity. That Harlow still thought herself surrounded by treachery and unfaithfulness, when servants and noblemen respected her so, when not even Snow could muster the strength to stop loving her.

Licking her lips, and suddenly tired, Snow declared, "It didn't last long." A short pause, and then, "Hating you, I mean; being angry. I am not very good at it, it seems, and it soon faded away so that all I had left was grief. Such grief, Harlow, because I still don't understand what compelled you–Are you so good at your games of shadows that I can't ever see you for what you are? I refuse to believe that Evil Queen nonsense."

Harlow reached forward minutely, as if she wanted to hold Snow's hands and then thought better of it. Instead, she placed both her hands flat against her ribcage until they were pale from the pressure.

"I have this darkness inside me," she murmured. "It is futile to deny that my desires don't run down wicked paths or that it doesn't feel good when my will is enforced."

Snow put her arms about herself, recoiling from Harlow and warming herself up with her own hands against her skin. She kneaded at her arms, felt goose bumps under her palms as she did. She was too exhausted to be angry, but a heavy sadness crawled up her throat as Harlow began to unravel the truths of her heart.

Her voice was defeated when she asked, "So you did truly desire my death?"

"No!" Harlow jumped as she exclaimed her word, emotion filling her voice so it rose and cracked.

She reached forward again, but Snow's hands were no longer available, so she was left with her own hovering in the air between them, lost. Snow watched Harlow's long fingers curl in on themselves and retreat, and fought herself to not follow their way and unlock them, so that they could hold hands and pretend there was nothing wrong between them.

"You heard them, didn't you? The fae behind my mirrors?" Harlow asked next, straightening up and trying to find her composure.

"Yes, I did."

"What did you hear exactly?"

"Laughter, butterflies, a terrible murmur. They seemed like ghosts to me, long-fingered and cruel." Snow could still feel them, in fact, lingering at the back of her mind, creeping up her spine and teasing her with fear, even when they had done her no harm and when she knew they were now far away.

"They sound like a song to me," Harlow countered. "Even now, they chant sweetly, they speak in whisper-like and soft tendrils… They speak in prophecy, they sing of what is to come…"

Snow watched as Harlow lost herself in her speech, her voice taking the quality of spell. She looked beautiful when she did, but the sight scared Snow, for Harlow was unapproachable like that, a creature not unlike the fairies she spoke about, of changing temperament and capricious wishes, one which Snow could never grasp and hold and keep close.

"Prophecy pulls us apart, my dear, and it speaks of a world divided for as long as we both dwell in it."

"And better me than you?" Snow snapped, more tired than angry.

Harlow shook her head, a continuous murmur of *no* parting her lips maddeningly as she brought both her hands up to her hair and buried them there, holding onto her curls and pulling. She looked like a lunatic, persecuted by voices only she could hear, her eyes now closed and her fingers tight, pulling, hurting. Snow had never wanted to understand her more than now, when her mysteries were not beautiful and alluring, but hurtful instead.

"I cannot say what I mean," Harlow said suddenly, turning about herself before settling once more in one spot and keeping still, her hands not leaving her hair.

"I killed your father, dear Snow, and if only for that you should hate me, but you refuse to do so even when my crimes have been far worse." Breathing harsh, but not daring to stop now that she had started Harlow confessed, "I tried to kill you, and for all that I regretted the choice a moment later, for all that I thought to myself that eternal sleep wasn't as terrible a punishment, that I had been forced by my circumstances, by prophecy and a kingdom that hated me… I tried to kill you, dear Snow, and it was my choice to do so. And how could you ever–how could you ever forgive me and say that you love me? How could I ever deserve your love after everything that I have been, everything that I still am? You call it nonsense, but I am indeed the Evil Queen."

"You can choose not to be so, and I… I…" Snow sighed, letting her wishes linger in the silence of the room. She was so very tired, and she didn't want to fight, or to face the truths of Harlow's speech.

Walking slowly, she made her way towards the bed and sat down heavily, dropping her weight as if dead. She looked upon Harlow, watched her anguish and her confusion, and dared to believe in her regret. She'd often been accused of naiveté, and perhaps she would be guilty of it by choosing to forgive Harlow's crimes. However so, weren't they all guilty of violence and revenge? Hadn't she allowed a war to break out and to corrode the kingdom because she'd been angry? They had been born the ruling class, and all they had done with their power had been to corrupt and to hurt. Couldn't she, then, forgive and move forward, hope for a future where none of them chose darkness?

"I won't forget, Harlow," Snow confessed, "but I could forgive and move past everything, so long as you promised to do so, too. We could, I don't know, I suppose… it might truly help if you told me what your intentions were in bringing me here at this time. Had you been planning to…" she stopped, lingered on her thoughts and blushed at the notion, "… seduce me?"

Harlow's hands came down at that, freeing her head from the pressure of her fingers and dropping by her sides, maybe tired, perhaps defeated, but at least calmer than a moment before, when madness had seemed to take hold of her. She shrugged, looking suddenly childish even when she was still worried, perhaps trapped by the notions of her singing fae and their terrible soothsaying.

A coy smile adorned Harlow's face, and she bit her lower lip before she said, "Hardly; but then you looked at me with your pretty eyes and such anticipation and I couldn't resist."

"But had you thought about it before?"

"I may have held the fantasy close to my heart, yes," Harlow confessed, dropping her shyness in favor of the sly smile of a seductress. She was so comfortable in her flirting, and Snow so wanted to get caught in her web.

Snow smiled as well, feeling lighter despite the heavy subject of their conversation, thinking that perhaps there was hope somewhere in their mutual revelations, in the shared knowledge of a past that had been cruel to them both, and had made them turn on each other.

"I didn't think you would hold such intentions when I agreed to this truce."

"What did you think, then, darling? That I should torture you, humiliate you, maybe kill you, after all?"

Snow shrugged, embarrassed, and knew herself and her intentions caught when Harlow barked out a quick, amused laugh.

"You didn't even think about it, did you?" Harlow wondered, her question needing no answer. "You signed off your freedom to your worst enemy, and didn't even think of what could happen to you."

“I was ever so tired of our war, and you did offer truce and reprieve; I hadn’t heard a better offer in years.”

Harlow sighed audibly after that, making a dramatic show out of the sound. She moved towards Snow and carefully took a seat next to her on the bed, keeping a small distance between them so that they wouldn’t be touching. Snow felt her anyway, her closeness and her heat, the flowery scent of her hair and the sound of her breathing gaining calmness with every intake. She looked at her and thought of their words and their pasts, and knew then that it would be easy to hate her, to heap vengeance upon her and curse her for an evil witch. She would have a kingdom and a prince at her side, and soon enough no one to oppose her. But then to think of life without Harlow, when she’d felt more alive in the past few days than she had in years, when her anger and her treasons would only make sense when next to Harlow and her own.

Harlow looked at her, too, lifting her head and leaning backwards as if she was too close and needed the distance. “I am sorry if I have crossed a line with you again. I thought you enjoyed sharing my bed, but I fear it has been one further mistake.”

“Wait, you think I don’t like it?” Snow wondered, surprised by the turn in the conversation. She had never been so sensually aware of her body, and had certainly never felt as intimate a pleasure as she had with Harlow. She’d thought that, at least, was clear as water between them.

“I thought you did, but then you cried after I–”

“That was because you were being a stubborn idiot!” Snow snapped, smiling when Harlow’s eyes widened impossibly, confusion obvious in the pretty hazel pools.

“Excuse me?”

"You came to me, high and mighty in your queenly ways, all ready to seduce me as some kind of power game for daring to question you! You refused to kiss me, or to let me touch you and you kept yourself away from me even as you touched me so intimately, and I… You hurt me with your dismissal."

"I thought I hurt you with my ties and my mirrors."

"I loved the ties," Snow confessed, the statement thoughtless yet truthful, and surely coating her cheeks in shades of bright red. "I didn't hate the mirrors."

"You did?"

Snow nodded, parting her lips as if to say something yet unsure of which words to choose. She wanted to say that she had dreamed of Harlow even before understanding what it was that she was dreaming about; that she had spent years thinking of the warmth of their thighs pressed together casually during the winter solstice bonfires; that she hadn't known pleasure until Harlow's fingers hadn't parted her legs; that all her wishes were for Harlow to allow her the bliss of touching her in return.

Bringing her hand up and curling it in the air, Snow put her knuckles to Harlow's cheek, her caress a barely-there touch of trembling fingers, the feeling of Harlow's skin less than a tease.

"I quiver at the thought of you, *cariño.*"

Harlow took Snow's hands from where it was resting against her cheek, curled her fingers about it until she was holding it and then forced it to open, so it was Snow's palm that was now cupping her face. She turned into the touch, nosing at Snow's palm and then kissing it softly, her lips nigh unnoticeable her brush was so soft. She closed her eyes and breathed in, lingering in the moment while Snow deepened the caress, bringing her thumb under Harlow's tired eyelids and drawing a gentle line with the pad of her finger.

"What is that which you called me?" Harlow wondered, her voice a whisper so that Snow almost missed the meaning of her words. "You have used that word before."

"*Cariño?*" Snow wondered, only now noticing her slip of the tongue, the ease with which the endearment had left her mouth. "It means darling; it's my mother's native tongue, Castilian. I never learned it, but some words remain."

"I like it," Harlow said, keeping her eyes closed still as if embarrassed by the admission. She smiled against the palm of Snow's hand, and then moved to look at her. "I would like to show you something, if you'd let me."

Snow nodded thoughtlessly, aware as she was of their proximity and the sudden intimacy of the words they had shared. She had the fleeting notion that Harlow was about to undress before her, so that when she stood, Snow felt her cheeks grow warm. Harlow didn't, however, and instead she offered her hand for Snow to take.

"Come, we shall take a stroll through the forest."

"Oh, somehow I had figured something completely different," Snow said, taking Harlow's hand anyway and following her suddenly insistent pull.

"Oh?" Harlow wondered as she guided her out of the rooms and past the entrance to the tower so that they could take the long climb down the stairs.

Breathless, Snow confessed, "I thought you were about to let me see you naked."

Harlow laughed gaily and stopped in her tracks, turning around and finding Snow's waist with her arm, so that they were locked in a sudden embrace. Snow fell into it, taking that one step that was separating her from Harlow and filling her frame with her own. She brought her arms up as well, around Harlow's shoulders so that they were face to face and breathing against each other.

Smiling, the gap between her teeth making her impossibly beautiful, Harlow said, "Maybe later, if you behave."

Snow leaned forward and kissed her, disposing of the shyness of the past and denying Harlow absolute control, demanding when before she hadn't dared ask. Harlow kissed back, lips soft in a gentle lock, barely more than a press of their mouths. It was good, anyway, just breathing against each other, small brushes of their lips bridging the gap that had pulled them apart these past few days. They still had a ways to go, but for now, Snow could live in this embrace and this kiss, in the sweetness of confession and the promise of a future.

"Oh, I dare say, Your Majesty, you will bring us down with your frolicking."

They pulled apart abruptly when Mrs. Agnes' voice interrupted their moment, Snow flushed all over and Harlow smiling, an amused tilt to her head as she regarded the head of household. Mrs. Agnes looked more entertained than she did shocked, and Snow had a moment to wonder how many times she'd caught Harlow kissing another woman in one of the palace's hallways.

"You did advise me to be nicer to the princess, did you not?" Harlow commented, tickled by Mrs. Agnes' show of disapproval.

"I'll keep away from doing so in the future, if I know what's good for me, Your Majesty," Mrs. Agnes replied, motioning then towards the stairs and instructing, "Off you go now, both of you. Keep away from trouble."

Harlow did as she was told, laughing as she grabbed Snow's hand and pulled her down the stairs.

"The only woman who dares command a queen," she stated, her giddiness bubbling over the words and her smile dispelling any notions of censure or discontent.

This same Harlow that now laughed with her head of household, much as one might with a dear aunt, would later claim that she was hated by all, and loved by none. Had her mother's wishes of revenge clouded her view of the world so much, or had the sacrifices she had made in her name built distrust within her? Perhaps only the fae and their whispers were to fault, for only when following their spell had Harlow proven to be terrible.

Harlow took them past the palace's gates with the same momentum that she'd kept to run down the stairs. They only stopped to gather coats and gloves, minding the cold of the midmorning, which teased at them with hints of sunrays filtering through the grey clouds, yet remained humid and uncomfortable. Two guards followed them silently, keeping their distance so that Snow found it easy to ignore them, and to instead enjoy the hint of cool dew on her face, and the feel of her hand inside Harlow's own, their gloves suddenly useless when Snow would have much preferred to feel Harlow's skin.

At the edge of the forest, they were left alone, both guards standing still where the trees began to grown thicker. Snow jumped a little then, and took hold of Harlow's arm, linking them together in a mockery of bosom buddies so as to walk closer to one another. They stumbled into each other as they strolled through the trees, both of them unused to such company, and suddenly diverted by walking side by side, their feet taking on the same rhythm.

They walked over the small river Snow loved so much and all the way to her favorite clear in the woods, where she had used to end her strolls back in the day. Harlow didn't stop there, however, and instead found hidden paths amongst the trees where human feet hadn't trailed often, so that the ground was full of twigs and rocks, and the leaves and branches loomed closer. Snow thought it enchanting, and as the light filtered here and there painting strange pictures against the greens and browns of the forest, she guessed that she would never be happier than walking through the woods next to Harlow.

Up a small hill and past a collection of summer trees, all of them naked of leaves and wearing nothing but their thin branches, Snow realized she was lost and would never be able to make her way back alone. A shiver run down her spine, not because she was afraid but because Harlow was walking her towards a secret, through places untouched by humans and inhabited by spirits of old. Snow laughed at the thought, and Harlow looked at her, amused.

"What is it, darling?"

"Should I perhaps be wary that you are bringing me through such unknown paths? I could never make my way back to the palace alone."

Snow's voice brimmed with joy and Harlow smiled at her, privy to the joke. She held on tighter all of a sudden, though, as if the mere suspicion that she bore ill-will towards Snow was a terrible thought. Snow clung back, moving her hand to rest on Harlow's arm and squeeze, reassuring her that she was exactly where she wanted to be.

They kept walking, and Snow was surprised to suddenly see a path of daffodils, their bright yellow and pinkish orange color a surprise against the greens, browns and whites of the forest in the winter. She opened her mouth and mumbled half a question that got lost in her excitement. She looked at Harlow, who was smiling as she dropped her arm and grabbed her hand instead, walking faster now and pulling her so that they were following the flowers. Soon, tulips appeared as well, and so did lilies and hyacinths, bluebells and peonies, a symphony of colors that belonged to the late spring, its warm weather and soft breeze.

As she walked through the flowers, a small pathway opening up in between them so that she felt invited inside a secret place, Snow heard water running, cascading even, the sound gushing and full. She looked up when the flowers gave way to fresh green grass, and saw a grove before her, a beautiful and low cascade running into a small pond and creating soft waves over the tranquil water. She heard birds and crickets and frogs, and all too suddenly realized that she was warm and that she could feel the sun on her face. She looked up, and saw the clear sky above her, summery blues blinking back at her when the sky had been grey for days now. She drew in a sharp breath and let go of Harlow's hand so she could twirl about herself and look at the place, this sweet, impossible secret of nature surrounding her in spring colors and the syrupy scent of flowers, making her ears hum with the soft buzzing of bees and the whooshing water of the cascade.

"What is this place?" Snow asked, marveled at the sight and not knowing where to let her gaze linger. She settled on the most luscious cluster of purple tulips for a moment, but then she just looked up again, at the clear skies.

"It's warm," she said, bringing her hands to her cheeks, and feeling her skin through her gloves. She took them off immediately and threw them to the grass, which once again caught her attention.

It was thick and bright green and all she wanted was to press her naked soles against it.

Harlow laughed when she spied her intentions, the sound climbing up graciously when Snow crouched down to untie her heavy winter boots and dropped them right next to her gloves.

"This is my secret grove," Harlow said. "I grew up here, and the fae still let me find it."

"They let you?" Snow wondered, pausing in midair as she struggled against her stockings, inelegantly pulling her skirts up past her knees to get to the lacing and do away with them. The heavy cotton was damp from the foggy atmosphere of the forest, and Snow still couldn't quite believe the warmth now making them uncomfortable.

Harlow laughed and held her when her antics made her trip on a loose stocking, and Snow smiled at her, prodding her again with, "You said the fae let you find this place."

"This place is magical, can't you feel it? It dangles somewhere in between our world and theirs and it is impervious to human exploration," Harlow explained, motioning around her as if to encompass the harmony and beauty that had gladly welcomed them. "It can only be found if such is the fae's wish."

"And they favor you so," Snow marveled, wondering about Harlow, a girl growing up in a magical land, her destiny and purpose only to leave it behind to play an ugly part in a terrible game of revenge.

"They let you in," Harlow murmured, now stepping away from her so that Snow could finish up undoing the laces of her stocking and push them down once and for all. "Perhaps it is not as I thought?"

Snow hummed, now only half an ear on what Harlow was saying. She pressed her feet, finally free, to the grass and stood up straight, closing her eyes and tilting her head up to catch the strange, magical sun. Warmth climbed up her feet and through her body, her feet rooting her to the ground below her, tingling where the soft grass touched her skin. The ground felt clean under her soles and it prickled gently at the skin. Snow breathed in once more and felt herself cocooned by the smell of dew and flowers in the spring. She hugged her arms about herself and listened to the water and the singing birds, and past them, to the magic singing in her ears, tickling at her senses. Where these the fairies that Harlow heard, this ancient, tranquil chant humming at the back of her neck? It was nothing like the ghostly presence of the mirror room. This felt gentle and careful.

Snow opened her eyes after a while, and her vision was blurry when she did, as if she'd just woken up from a very long dream. She felt content, and she hummed under her breath as her eyes focused and searched for Harlow. She found her across the small pond, smiling down at three sparrows at her feet, twitting as if to keep her attention. She too had rid herself of her gloves, her shoes and her stockings, but also of her coat and her dress, her corset and her shift. She was standing naked under the sun, a few strands of thick hair now loose and falling carelessly over her neck and shoulders, and escaping her thick braid.

Snow breathed in slowly, turning away from the sun and the sky to stare at Harlow unashamedly. She followed the thin slope of her shoulders, her lovely arms and looked at her breasts, small and bouncing when she moved, dark brown nipples crowning her golden skin. She had wide hips and a small belly, skin stretching gently around her bellybutton, making her plump and soft-looking so that Snow imagined laying her head down on her stomach, feeling the slight slope of flesh and resting there forever. Further down she spied a bush of thick copper hair and she blushed, thinking of what lay under, of Harlow's softest, wet skin, of the folds and secrets at the apex of her thighs. She couldn't stare for long, but she let her eyes linger on Harlow's long legs, her strong thighs and shapely ankles. She didn't look delicate but she did look magnificent, a creature that belonged to this impossible nature that was warm in the middle of winter.

Harlow moved her arms up to unpin her hair, her movements precise. Snow kept on staring, taking notice only now of the strange colors tinting her skin, pinks, reds and yellows splotched here and there and moving with her limbs. Snow leaned forward, feeling silly because Harlow remained across the pond and the movement did nothing to further Snow's exploration. The colors were there, nonetheless, distinct and beautiful on Harlow's skin and, Snow suddenly realized, painting flowers and leaves on her body. Rose petals cascaded past her left breast and down her torso, twisted as if blown by the wind; a fully blossomed marigold painted her belly dark orange as it rested right next to her bellybutton; pink, purple and white lilies danced across her right hip and thigh, loose petals traveling to the small of her back. The flowers were painted in soft strokes of color, as if put there by the most talented painter, who had found a canvas in Harlow's beautiful flesh. Snow only thought to ask about it once Harlow was done with her hair, now loose and falling down her back. However, Harlow moved forward with a little jump and then dived into the pond, her limbs graceless and a careless peal of laughter betraying childish glee.

Snow laughed too when Harlow came back up for air, pushing her hair back and exposing her torso, flowers, skin and bouncy breasts the most gorgeous sight Snow had ever seen.

"Come now, and stop staring already," Harlow ordered, smiling and bringing her hand forward as if to force Snow into the water.

Snow walked until she could dip her toes into the water, and smiled when she felt the warmth. "It's warm."

She started removing her clothes as well, dropping her thick coat to the green grass below and stretching herself as she did to catch the sun on her skin as it came free. She fought buttons and lacings, and sighed contentedly when her corset hit the ground. Once naked, she didn't dither and took the plunge, jumping into the water with a squeal, and smiling through the splash. She came up laughing, and opened her eyes to see Harlow's brilliant smile.

"So this is where you hide all the time," Snow stated, laughing still and looking about her at the moving water, at the small cluster of water lilies and the frogs jumping here and there.

"And people think I'm cavorting with evil spirits," Harlow answered, smiling so Snow felt no malice.

"The same people that believe I talk to birds, I should think."

"Oh, don't you? What a disappointment, dear Snow, that you don't prance the woods singing with the critters. The children of the court will be ever so disenchanted; they do love the notion, and Mrs. Agnes loves teasing them with it."

Snow waded her way towards Harlow slowly, smiling. Her feet didn't touch the ground and she wasn't a great swimmer, so she took her time. She felt small fish by her feet and ankles, and giggled when they swam too fast so that she felt tickles. She finally reached the center of the pond and Harlow, and feeling welcome, she immediately perched herself in between Harlow's arms, holding on to her shoulders both for support and because she wanted to be nowhere else. Harlow held her by the waist, and kept them close inasmuch as the movement of the water allowed.

"This is beautiful," Snow said. "Thank you for showing me."

Harlow's answer was a kiss, which Snow readily returned. It brought them closer, and suddenly Snow wished they weren't underwater, so that she could feel Harlow's body against hers without the slick sensation of the water all around them. She loved it, nonetheless, the awareness of naked skin, of the shape of her and the way their bodies met, hips and legs and breasts pressed together as they hadn't been before.

Harlow moved back abruptly, and Snow had no time to complain as Harlow sunk down and pulled her underwater. Snow opened her eyes and saw Harlow's hair flowing softly before her, pulled up by the water. She met Harlow's lips again, and laughed carefully against her mouth as momentum pulled them up and above the water. They repeated the motion, and kissed and kissed, water sloshing about them and flowers sticking to their skin as they came down and up again, as they broke apart and splashed each other, laughing breathlessly as they tired each other with passion and mirth.

They left the water eventually, and both of them flopped on the ground still laughing and breathing hard. The laid down side by side, and Snow closed her eyes as they did, taking in the moment. The magical sun touched her skin everywhere, quickly drying away the water clinging to her, yet the grass felt cool under her back. She felt grounded, laying down like this, close to the earth and maybe even a part of it, flimsy breeze awakening her every pore, and all her body aware of itself, bones and skin and flesh.

Her arm touched Harlow's casually, their hands knocking together as if by accident, and like this, they breathed in at the same time, working in unison, two whole beings finding the sort of peace that they had never allowed each other. Snow wondered, fleetingly, whether they would have found this sooner had Harlow denied the darkness threatening them outside of this place, back in the real world where the forests were cold and where they had brought a war upon their peers. She would never know now, and there was no point in mulling over such questions if what she wanted was to have a future next to Harlow – Harlow in peace, content, willing to trust her and their bond no matter what her mirrors whispered when Snow wasn't listening.

Eyes closed and breaths slowing down, Snow was tempted to give in to sleep. She wasn't tired, but she felt lazy and content, and felt that she would sleep far better here than she had back at the palace. Nonetheless, a different kind of temptation made her open her eyes and turn on her side. She rested her weight on her elbow to bring her head up and stare down at Harlow next to her, naked still and breathing slowly as well, her eyes closed and her limbs stretched as if to catch the sun, her hair in disarray over the green grass, its deep red color a beautiful contrast. Snow looked at her body all over again, delighted at the chance. She brought a hand up and let it hover over Harlow's side, wary of touching, yet full of anticipation. Harlow had touched her and loved her, she had pleasured her and watched her in ecstasy, yet Snow hadn't had an opportunity to do the same, so that being here, like this, only a breath away, somehow managed to be more intimate than Harlow's fingers caressing her insides.

Aware of her own nervousness, Snow swallowed visibly, and still with her hand poised in the air, ready to touch, she asked, "What are these?"

Harlow moved her face in the direction of her voice, but she kept her eyes closed. She only hummed for an answer, her tone questioning. Snow let her hand fall down then, carefully placing the pads of her fingers on Harlow's side, one by one below her breast, where a petal was painted over the tan skin.

"These?" Snow repeated. "The flowers?"

"They just appeared," she answered, her voice dreamy. "Slowly, over a few days, after my mom died. I believe they were a gift, an homage, perhaps, a celebration?"

"The fae gave them to you."

Harlow opened her eyes at half mast, smiling up at Snow and taking her hand to guide it over her skin. She brought Snow's fingers, delicate and loose in Harlow's grip, to a petal on her breast, framing her nipple, and let them rest there. She moved Snow's hand over the trail of color, down the slope of her breast and her side, to her hip where lilies blossomed.

"My mom's name was Lily Rose," Harlow whispered, moving then Snow's hand so that it rested on her belly, by her bellybutton. "And my aunt–"

"Marigold?"

"Yes."

"They are so beautiful," Snow repeated, somewhat in awe, thinking that perhaps Harlow belonged to the fae in ways she would never belong to the human world, after all. Would that make their affair impossible? Would Harlow, after all, choose the fae that gave her magic and flowers, even when the price they asked for in exchange was Snow's blood?

Harlow left Snow's hand resting by her belly, and brought her own up to touch Snow's cheek, cupping it so that Snow's attention was brought back to Harlow's sleepy eyes.

"What are you thinking, darling?" Harlow wondered.

"What will happen when our truce ends, Harlow? Tell me the truth."

Harlow waited a moment, her thumb soft as it drew circles on Snow's skin, and Snow didn't push. It wasn't long before Harlow said, "There will be a blood moon on the night our truce ends; it will be a time of sacrifice, where the veils between the worlds blur so that anything is possible. Our choices will be sealed by magic during that night, so that our deal will hold true; I shall vanish and be forgotten, and you should rule."

"What if I choose to stay with you?"

"We shall see what the spells of the blood moon bring, but let us not dwell on it now."

"Harl–"

"Kiss me, won't you, darling?"

"Are you going to avoid all conversations with kisses?"

"I will certainly try. Now do as you're told; I'm the queen and you're my prisoner, so get to it, princess dear."

Snow laughed and kept on smiling as she let Harlow guide her down. She pressed her lips to hers, feeling giddy when the motion moved her so that she was laying half on top of Harlow, their warm skin meeting and their limbs tangling carefully as they kissed. Harlow tasted clean, and she parted her lips under Snow's hungrily, drawing her closer with deep, long touches, her mouth and teeth playing around her chin and neck only to come back quickly, and keep kissing.

Harlow was lazy under her, so Snow took her time, happy to remain close and feeling Harlow's skin for the first time, slick next to her own, growing sweaty where they were pressed together. Her leg slipped between Harlow's casually, and Harlow kept her there, bending her knee and wrapping her thigh about Snow's hip to hold her close. Snow felt the soft skin against her, Harlow's fleecy hair pressing against her thigh, the wetness growing between her legs soon undeniable. She kept her movements slow, nonetheless, enjoying the feel of warm dampness against her skin, discovering for the first time the sticky, wet secrets between Harlow's legs, excited by finally getting a taste of Harlow's attraction. That she could give pleasure and not just receive it, that Harlow felt for her just as she felt for Harlow, that it wasn't just her body being teased into the realm of utter delight, it all might have been enough to keep Snow right where she was forever.

Forever was far too long, however, and after long moments of kissing and touching softly, of feeling her way around Harlow's body, Snow moved back, straddling Harlow's hips and looking down at her, hair messy on the green grass, flushed cheeks and body slick with perspiration and the remnants of water. Harlow smiled up at her, her lips taking on an impudent if lazy curve, the gap between her teeth making her look all the more beautiful. She let her arms fall to her sides as well, letting Snow's eyes roam freely over her skin, making it seem as if she were offering herself as sacrifice to the goddess above her. Snow laughed at the notion, feeling giddy and aroused and happy.

She stared at Harlow's chest, her small breasts moving up and down with her breathing, the slope of them beautiful in between her thin shoulders and sharp collarbones, nipples dusky, round, so very pretty. It occurred to her that Harlow was rather small when it came to it, that it was her otherworldly presence what made her seem so imposing. She was relaxed now, though, pliant under Snow's stare, all the more attractive for it.

"Are you going touch me, or are you just going to stare?"

Snow smiled, recognizing the tease for what it was, yet reading Harlow's impatience as well. "Would you let me just stare?"

"If you'd like, but then, I don't know that I would feel so generous next time."

Snow lied down to steal a kiss, smiling into it and then coming back up again, keeping her hands splayed on the grass so that she was bracketing Harlow's body with her own. She was nervous at the thought of touching her, now that she had been given the chance.

"I'm not sure I know how–"

"You can do no wrong in this, Snow."

Harlow smiled up at her, and once again taking the lead, she reached down for Snow's hands and brought them up to her own chest, letting them rest there softly. She pressed careful fingers to the light bruises on Snow's wrists, and then stopped touching them altogether. Snow enjoyed the pressure of Harlow's hands on her, and even more, she enjoyed the feel of her chest under her palms. She cupped her breasts securely now, drawing their shape with her fingers and then pressing her palms fully on them, feeling the tip of Harlow's nipples hard under her skin. She molded her hands over them once again, and pressed them close together, letting her thumbs reach for her nipples. She drew a circle about them, and moaned softly after Harlow took a deep breath, unwittingly forcing her chest up and closer to Snow's hands.

Snow leaned down, swallowing her excitement back and brushing her lips carefully against one of Harlow's nipples, getting a feel for it, finding the skin uneven but soft, surprisingly taut at the tip. She tasted it with her tongue, and when Harlow's breath became suddenly loud, she let herself play with the skin as she wanted. She pressed kisses around the bud, moving from one to the other until the skin was wet with saliva. She sucked on them, carefully, slowly, listening to Harlow's sounds of pleasure, finding the right way to touch, content when every single lick and kiss sent a jolt of pleasure straight to her own core. She hadn't known touching someone else could be such delight, not even when she'd dreamed of touching Harlow.

Harlow buried her hands in Snow's curls, holding on, and Snow left her chest to explore further. She brought her mouth up and her hands down, kissing at Harlow's collarbones as her hands glided down her sides, stroking softly. Harlow laughed against her and squirmed, the dance of their hips pressed together making Snow suddenly aware that she was wet, and probably coating Harlow's skin in sweat and arousal.

"I'm ticklish," Harlow complained, pulling at Snow's hair until Snow was laughing, too.

"The Evil Queen's weakness! You'll never defeat me now!"

Snow dug her fingers in harder, eliciting a loud peal of laughter and stopping Harlow from uttering any more words she was laughing so hard. They struggled amongst giggles, and only stopped when Harlow freed her hand and slapped Snow's ass hard, making her groan immediately.

Laughter still clinging to her eyes, Harlow wondered, "Did you like that? Now there's a possibility."

Dropping her weight forward and her mouth to Harlow's neck, Snow groaned again, circling her hips unwittingly to the rhythm of Harlow's palm on her ass, now softly stroking the spot she had slapped. Her skin would be red, she had no doubt, and she bit her lip thinking of asking Harlow to make it redder, and then to kiss it better.

"Some other day," she whispered, pressing a kiss to the skin of Harlow's neck, tempted to leave a bruise herself. She had other plans, though, so she said, "I want…"

She let the words linger, biting her lips she was so embarrassed at speaking her mind. Which was silly, because they were naked and wet and rubbing against each other, their hips moving of their own accord, gracelessly looking for pleasure and release.

"I want…" she repeated, trailing her hand down Harlow's side, this time pressing hard against the skin to avoid tickling. She let it rest by her hip briefly, and then trailed lower, past her bellybutton and over her mound, to where her hair turned wiry.

"Whatever you want, please, darling."

Snow looked up and searched for Harlow's eyes, saw them dark and round and beautiful, her expression open, and trusting. She wanted a kiss and she didn't stop herself from getting one, sliding up to catch Harlow's lips with her own and parting her mouth as she did, so that their tongues met with abandon. She stayed in the kiss for a moment, wet breathing harsh in between them as they broke apart and came together again, chasing the feeling of their mouths pressed together, of teeth against lips and tongues caressing each other.

After a time, however, Snow slid down Harlow's body, guiding her movement with her mouth and leaving kisses as she went, drawing a wet line in between her breasts and down her torso, all the way to her bellybutton and past it, until she was settled between her legs. Her hands remained up, under Harlow's breasts so that her fingers were resting on them, absentmindedly catching a nipple as they moved. Harlow trapped them there with her own hands, and parted her legs wider so that Snow rested more comfortably in between, her shoulders bracketed by Harlow's thighs, the skin there taut and muscular, its beautiful tan painted in sweat and the strange pale pink color of the lilies traveling her body. Snow turned her head to place a kiss against a bunch of loose petals painted on the inside of Harlow's thigh, the taste of perspiration unfamiliar and sweet. She stayed there a moment, feeling the slick skin under her lips and inhaling the strong scent of Harlow's arousal, tangy and alluring.

Snow buried her nose between Harlow's wet, curly hair, and closed her eyes, breathing in the scent of her, of her sweat and her skin, of her flesh quivering beneath her lips. She leaned up and forward to place a sweet kiss on Harlow's mound, right where her hair started to grow, and smiled when Harlow groaned above her, the sound accompanied by her thighs and hips moving together, rolling closer and seeking attention. Snow mouthed her way through her skin without knowledge, letting her instincts guide her past Harlow's outer lips and in to her pussy, to the pink, stretched flesh before her. She flattened her tongue against Harlow's opening and licked at her without expertise, moaning unwittingly at the foreign flavor of her, at the rubbery soft feeling of her damp skin.

Snow kept at it, experimenting with her tongue, reading Harlow's moans and pushing and pulling as she went, enjoying every moment of being buried between her legs. She held on to

Harlow's thighs, circling them with her arms and hands and grounding herself, digging her nails in when Harlow moaned at the rough treatment. She kissed Harlow's skin over and over again, licking inside her and gathering the taste, feeling fire course through her veins when she sucked at the pretty, reddish nub demanding attention and Harlow shivered in between her arms. She established no pace, but soon they were both moving together, Harlow's hips making an effort to match the cadence of Snow's tongue.

"Darling…" Harlow whispered, her voice lingering in the air and becoming louder, not words but moans leaving her parted lips.

Snow breathed slowly as she touched her, feeling every sound and every touch, aware of the grass under her body, the soft caress of the sun against her back, and above all aware of Harlow, skin and scent and sound, her body rolling its way into pleasure. Snow stretched her tongue inside her and licked carefully, collecting her taste before she mouthed her way back to her clit and latched onto it, using her teeth briefly and smiling when Harlow groaned.

"Again," Harlow demanded above her, her tone firm even through her breathlessness, unbearably hot so that it made Snow's skin buzz, pleasure pooling in her belly so that it was hard to concentrate.

She followed Harlow's orders, though, and bit and sucked gently on her sensitive skin, relentlessly now, wanting her to come apart under her mouth, wanting to be responsible for her pleasure. Harlow helped herself, burying her hands in Snow's hair to keep her close and letting her feet leave the ground so as to wrap herself completely about Snow, her heels digging themselves in her back, her body a hot wire of tension. Snow felt enveloped by her, by her bliss and her flesh, by her muscles strained with anticipation even as her wet core rested so pliantly against her tongue. Snow felt sensual, wild, consumed by Harlow's sex and desire.

Harlow's muscles tightened when she came, yet her pussy trembled under Snow's tongue, her flesh pulsing with pleasure. Snow moaned at the feeling of her and kissed her through it all, keeping her lips pressed sweetly against the reddish, puffy skin of her folds, lingering there even as Harlow's thighs unlocked and her feet fell to the ground, legs spread inelegantly around Snow. Snow moved her hands up, searching for her sweaty skin and cupping her breasts, climbing then up her body and dropping messy kisses here and there. Harlow squirmed, her skin too sensitive now and suddenly ticklish, but smiled wider with every kiss and caress, trying to embrace Snow to bring her closer.

Snow fell half on top of Harlow and half on the ground, and Harlow moved about to fit her in her hold, bringing their chests together and their mouths close, and slyly pressing her thigh between Snow's legs. Snow moaned softly, quietly, whatever control she'd mastered while in between Harlow's legs now gone and substituted by quivering need.

"Oh, I'm so–so–"

"Wet."

Harlow's voice was hoarse, sensual, and the tone traveled as if a physical touch down Snow's skin. She was so aroused it nearly hurt. Harlow pushed up with her thigh, bending her knee and using her hips so that her supple skin pressed harder on Snow's core.

"Come, let me see your pleasure."

Harlow brought her hand to her ass, encouraging Snow to move against her, to ride her as she needed. Snow did, feeling out of sorts and too far gone to think past the feeling of Harlow beneath her, of their breasts pressed together, nipples thrust close and sensitive against their slick skin, of her mouth so close and so beautiful, of her eyes still dark. She kissed Harlow to ground herself, and she felt dirty and happy and loved, the cresting wave of pleasure making her feel giddy. Their messy, breathless kiss continued past Snow's breaking point, swallowing her small moans and bringing her down.

Time moved slowly like molasses for the rest of the afternoon, their kisses easing them down from pleasure only to fire them up again, their bodies gravitating together and refusing to break apart. Snow allowed Harlow to maneuver her in to bliss, blushing when she beckoned her to straddle her face, encouraging her with deep moans when she pressed their cores together, wet folds sliding together and their legs tangled impossibly, the feeling not nearly enough yet so very intimate that Snow never wanted to let go. They kissed and prodded and loved each other, and as the magic sun of the grove set, they bathed in warm water once more, and lastly laid down on the grass, staring up at the sky as their arms touched and their fingers played with each other.

"You ruined me, I believe," Snow said after she had recovered her breath, her word the first coherent ones she'd spoken in hours.

Harlow laughed, obviously content. Snow looked at the way her breasts bounced with her happiness, her pretty brown nipples still a little peaked and almost tempting Snow into beginning their lovemaking all over again. She reached out and traced a painted petal on Harlow's ribs, still fascinated by the strange colors on her skin, and was just about to touch further when her stomach complained loudly. Harlow laughed even harder.

"I fear our skipping lunch is taking a toll; it's nearly dinner time," Harlow said.

"Notions of time seem so very odd in this place."

"We should eat, nonetheless; Mrs. Agnes will have my head if I let you go hungry, and I do think she's planned that wonderfully tasty sauce for the mutton today."

Snow hummed, the notion of food appealing and her stomach growling at the mention of mutton. She smiled, thinking of sitting by Harlow and amongst the court, eating and drinking and laughing, of a quiet night by the fire, and of finding sleep in Harlow's bed.

"Come, let's not delay any further."

Snow followed Harlow's orders, standing up heavily and letting Harlow help her into her gown and her coat, and then helping her back, laces and buttons proving far more difficult when being fastened, rather than unfastened. They still looked a mess when they stepped away from the grove, hair uncombed and wild, dresses a little crooked in places and skin dry from sweat and water, all traces of lip stain and perfume gone from their bodies and substituted by a healthy blush and the scent of spring flowers.

They walked back hand in hand, and as they strolled through the winter forest, once again cold and shrouded by the darkness of the wintry night, Snow wondered whether she would ever cross this forest again and find the secret grove. These forests had been friend and foe, and she couldn't help but think of running scared through them during a night not unlike this one, fearing Harlow's wrath. She looked at their joined hands to keep her thoughts at bay, and held on to the hope that they could share a future of beauty, trust and love.

Once they had crossed the limits of the forest and were walking towards the palace, Harlow said, "Lady Roslyn promised she would sing for us tonight, it will be good fun."

Snow hummed knowingly and countered, "You only like Lady Roslyn because she pushes her huge breasts up in impossible dresses for you."

"And very nice breasts they are," Harlow deadpanned next to her, smiling and squeezing her hand. "If she should push them up for someone, then surely it should be her queen."

"There seems to be no lack of offers to fill your bed, am I right? Men and women of the court will gladly take up the position of royal consort."

There was no maliciousness in Snow's prodding, if there was curiosity. That Harlow hadn't remarried had always been a running commentary, one that hadn't done her any favors and which had only furthered the notion of her cavorting with demons. That she kept many lovers had always been a malicious notion of the kingdom's tongues, yet Snow hadn't known her to keep any, at least not publicly. That she hardly lacked for offers, well, that was no secret.

Harlow squeezed her hand once more, and then moved so that it was their arms that were locked and they were walking like close chums. "Should I have no offers? They do say I am that fairest of them all, and that I might even go to war over the notion."

Snow guffawed, "Silly, though it's true you are the fairest."

Harlow stopped them in their tracks then, even as they stood a breath away from the palace's entrance and Snow could already taste the warmth of the hearth. Harlow kissed her, long and greedy, out where anyone could see. Her lips were cold from the wind and Snow strived to warm them up, prolonging the kiss and keeping still inside Harlow's arms, cherishing the closeness.

"My bed has been empty for years now, if that is what you're asking," Harlow said when they broke apart.

Snow shook her head, feeling suddenly childish. There was a war being fought outside this palace, she had a husband and a kingdom of her own, and her standing with Harlow was nothing if not unsure and possibly dangerous. She shouldn't be thinking about love and a warm bed, she shouldn't be hoping that she and Harlow would fall into each other yet again tonight, and she most certainly shouldn't be wondering about the lovers Harlow may have taken once upon a time.

"It's not," she answered. "It is simply that I do not know where we stand, Harlow, and whether we stand together or not, despite everything; and that all I should be thinking about is your mouth upon me…"

The feeling of Harlow's gloved hand on her cold cheek was barely comforting, but Snow still leaned into it as it was offered, and breathed in the smell of soft wool.

"Give me a little time, darling, and I shall share my secrets."

"But you robbed us of time, Harlow. There is a decision to be made on the night the moon is full, and I fear you haven't told me everything about it."

"I have not," Harlow confessed, looking up at the moon as Snow unwittingly did the same.

Snow wished for time to stop, for the moon to remain blue and pretty and still, so that she could have this moment in time forever. Yet she knew her wish to be selfish, for the winter was hard and the war had taken its toll, and the people of their kingdoms deserved peace more than Snow deserved comfort.

"It won't be long now, dear Snow, and no matter the outcome this war will be over, our feud will be forgotten, and the fairy folk will stop playing games, I promise."

Snow nodded, and when her stomach growled again, she forgot her worries and laughed instead. "I am so hungry."

"Let's solve that first, then."

Days of bliss followed, only marred by the notion that they were living on borrowed time. Snow held to her joy all the tighter for it, trying to quiet Harlow's occasional turns into brooding with passion and laughter, hoping to hear her worries and deem them unimportant. Harlow refused to share further though, and so Snow was left dangling alone in her anticipation, sure that the pact Harlow had spoken at the battlefield hadn't been made casually. Harlow often talked of prophecy, after all, and now more than ever Snow wondered at the hidden paths the fairy folk had drawn for her.

However so, Snow tasted what life might be like next to Harlow, in this palace of her childhood that had once been full of gloom. It was not so now, despite the heavy ordeal that had brought her here. Instead, Snow realized that she could be happy here, as Harlow's companion, as a willing, wanted member of this household, even as a useful part of the governing council Harlow trusted. She would never be a stateswoman, of that she was sure, but she was keen to learn and enjoyed sitting by Harlow when she partook in council with her court. Snow listened and spoke candidly at times, borrowing from her heart more than she did from her intellect, yet receiving interest in her speech. The members of the council took to her quickly once she showed an interest in matters of state, and they seemed to agree that she was a clear influence in Harlow's mind and that she mellowed her harsher instincts.

Nonetheless, Snow still enjoyed stories far more than she enjoyed treaties and state papers. Harlow opened her library to her with a smile, and Snow perused it with as much enthusiasm as she did the forests, surprising unsuspecting court members when they found her sprawled on the floor, the pretty fabrics of her gowns spread all around her and her shoes forgotten somewhere by a pile of books. Harlow laughed at her disorder and at the way the members of the court would shake her head at her, as if she were an unruly but amusing child. Snow remembered that feeling well, that notion of simple love and acceptance that she had known when she'd lived here in the past, the warmth of being wanted.

In this palace, Snow had the view of the sky from her mother's window, books and the forests to explore, Harlow's company at dinner, in bed, by her side so long as she asked for it, and the simple pleasure of no one thinking her dim-witted when she walked about shoeless, when she stared dreamily outside, when she sat upon a table. It felt like home, like a promising future, like beauty and joy and wonder. And if not for Harlow's doubts, for her flaring temper and for the secrets hidden within her mirror room, Snow may have been fooled into complete delight. She was no idiot, nor naïve, though, and she couldn't afford to forget her and Harlow's past, lest they repeat it. They had a war and a blood feud between them, and only their own hearts to fight it – and hers beat steadily now, sure of what it wanted, yet Harlow's remained a mystery.

Harlow had a tortured mind, and sharing her bed had let Snow see her at her most vulnerable. Harlow was far from a heavy sleeper, and she often woke in the middle of the night, more than once, and paced the room mindlessly, her eyes settled in the worlds behind the mirrors, the ones only she could see. Bathed by the moonlight, in translucent nightgowns when not naked, she was a witch, a sorceress, yet not a creature of evil. She worried, she gnawed at her lip, she pulled her hair, and sometimes she talked back to voices only she could hear. Snow heard no one reply, yet she did hear a buzzing of sorts, the murmuring giggle of what she now knew were the fairy folk. She wondered at the words they whispered, and both pitied and adored Harlow for being able to understand them.

On their third night together, when awoken by Harlow's soft steps and the singing murmur of magical creatures, Snow left the bed as naked as Harlow herself. Snow jumped on the cold stone floor, uncomfortable, and made her way to Harlow, blocking her view of the standing mirror by plastering herself to its surface, her back pressing against the crystal. She hoped her skin would stain the surface, make it blurry.

"What are you–"

"Shhh, *cariño*, you need to rest, you must stop looking."

Harlow didn't stop looking, but it wasn't the fairies that called for her attention now, but Snow herself. Snow had only noticed the pull she had on Harlow's attention on the past few days, the way Harlow searched for her among a crowd, the way her eyes would fix themselves on her and never leave. She'd been so sure she was the one looking for Harlow all the time that she'd never noticed that Harlow was looking for her in return.

"Come," Snow offered, bringing her arms forward and opening them around her body, offering comfort, offering herself.

Harlow had a moment of doubt, but she didn't deny her, walking into her embrace and hiding her face against the hollow of her neck. They were both cold, and they pressed closer together, trying to find warmth in the touch of the bodies.

"Tell me what they say, what you're always hearing."

Harlow shook her head, the sharp movement made less harsh by her hands on Snow's hips, her hold sure but soft and her touch wandering down her thighs and to her back, to where Snow's ass rested against the mirror.

"Did we not decide I should be the one giving the orders? I do recall a deal."

Harlow came away from her hiding spot with a smile, small but amused, a sure sign that she was trying to forget her turmoil. Snow smiled back, leaned closer and stole a kiss.

"Punish me for my terrible behavior, then."

"No, not tonight."

Harlow reached down for Snow's hands as she spoke, and took them between hers. She brought them up to her mouth and kissed Snow's wrists, now marred by fresh reddish bruises, the signs of last night burning still on her skin. Snow had begged to be tied up, and Harlow had been ever so careful, making sure it was Snow's desire to be so subjugated, and not a strange influence of their pact.

"What, then?" Snow prodded, amused, already wet, strangely aroused by the mirror at her back, now warm from her own skin. She wanted her sweat plastered on it, the smell of her desire pressed to the scentless surface, and she wanted Harlow to look at it and think of her, naked and wanting, and not of prophecy or magic.

Harlow smiled, leaning closer as if to kiss her and then denying her the pleasure, breathing against her parted lips, her humid and warm breath tempting. In the darkness of the room, pressed up as they were, the intimacy of the gesture made Snow's heart beat harder, her breathing come a little sort. She was already sweating with anticipation and she smiled, having only wanted to pull Harlow back to bed for a spot of sleep, but happy for the alternative.

When Harlow didn't move, Snow searched for that kiss, leaning forward and catching her mouth at the last moment. She laughed as the awkward connection turned comfortable and familiar, as Harlow bit her bottom lip. Snow felt warmer now, but only by virtue of Harlow's touch, so that when Harlow went down to her knees, she missed her instantly. The sight of Harlow kneeling stopped her from protesting, however. She laughed, instead, when Harlow pressed a row of kisses to her hipbone, where she was most ticklish. She squirmed away playfully, but she was trapped by the mirror behind her, so she only wiggled this way and that, so that Harlow's kisses landed on her stomach, under her bellybutton, at the top her thighs, where the skin was sensitive and responsive, already warm from the soft touches.

Harlow steadied her after a moment of play, caressing the back of her thighs with a firm touch and settling her hands at the back of her knees. Snow shivered at the new touch, ticklish and thrilling both.

"You're trembling," Harlow murmured, mumbling the words against the skin of her belly.

"I just like it when you touch me."

Harlow's answer was a deep hum, the vibration of her lips as she pressed soft kisses all around awakening Snow's skin, making her hairs stand on end. Harlow took little time to find the wet flesh between her legs, however, foregoing teasing in favor of quick, hard caresses of her tongue, her mouth searching for Snow's pleasure hungrily. She ate her out quietly, and Snow barely breathed harshly as fire burnt her core and traveled over her skin, her knees trembling where Harlow was holding on to them and her hands searching for something to grasp. She held on to the mirror behind her and it cricked, the wooden frame complaining and keeping up a monotonous rickety sound when she moved her hips to the cadence of Harlow's tongue.

Her pleasure came fast, but it was languid and it licked at her insides in warm strokes. Harlow held her as her legs refused to keep her up, her hands traveling up again, from her knees and up the back of her thighs, holding steady to her ass as she slid down the mirror and to the floor. Snow laughed once she was in Harlow's arms. She looked back at the mirror and saw her figure now blurred on the surface in sweaty lines. She could see the roundness of her ass and the strong shape of her thin shoulders, now shadowing the worlds behind it.

"Makes for a better view, I suppose," Harlow said, amused if not unworried, her tired eyes still showing the strain from lack of sleep and tumultuous thoughts.

"Let's sleep, please; the sun will be up in no time," Snow whined, stealing a kiss because she could, and because she wanted to mellow Harlow down and trick her to go back to bed.

Harlow didn't oppose her, and they stood up lazily and walked back to bed, quickly diving under the thick covers and searching for warmth. They met in the middle of the bed and cuddled together, and even if the morning would find them spread apart and looking for their own space, they fell asleep close together, breathing in sync.

The next day saw them traveling together in a carriage, the muddy ground making the journey uncomfortable and slow. Harlow was uncomfortable, too, and Snow felt tense, her nerves feeding off from Harlow's own. It had been the Military Advisor's idea that they should travel together to the main village before the

Royal Estate, a rousing speech of good faith and togetherness convincing Harlow to take on a task that she would have gladly avoided.

The palace had been sending supplies steadily towards the kingdom's villages all throughout the winter, the war having taken a toll and Harlow having pulled her court's resources together to help her people as much as possible. She had a keen mind for business, too, Snow had noticed, and her commercial trading seemed impeccable and iron-clad. She remembered her years of war as a time of struggle and strife, and now wondered whether Charles should have been as attentive to the kingdom's finances as he'd been to the war. His mother had spared no expense towards the war, as well, and Snow had let the details go over her head, happy to let them rule and fight her battles.

Apparently, Harlow's advisors had been wanting her to make an appearance before her people for a time now, to pay a candid visit without her armor and her magic. People were ever so afraid of her, of her sorcery and her abrasiveness, after all, and Snow had agreed that seeing her as a caring figure would perhaps begin to dispel the hatred of the people. That Snow should join her hadn't been questioned, when surely seeing them standing together and Snow in good health would put them both in a different light. Mrs. Agnes had told Snow that rumors in town were that she had been made a true prisoner, and that Harlow continued to mistreat her.

The day had risen cloudy, and the winter morning was cold, but the inside of the carriage felt cramped and stuffy. They were both covered in thick winter gowns and coats, Harlow's red hair a clashing match to the purple satin interior of the carriage, and the heavy tiara she had insisted on wearing making her look lost behind her own queenly image. Tension rolled off of her in waves, and after a time, Snow reached forward and for her hand, opening her fist and squeezing her fingers. She was met with sweaty, cold skin, as if Harlow were about to break a fever.

Snow kept on squeezing, adding pressure as she went and hoping to meet Harlow's eyes. Harlow allowed the touch, but remained passive within it and refused to meet her gaze, keeping her eyes wide open and firmly settled on the road outside. Snow too looked outside after time, watching the trees pass by them slowly. Joined by nothing but their hands, Snow still felt close to Harlow, and wished to comfort her uneasiness. She worried, too, for Harlow looked like the infamous Evil Queen as she sat before her, and Snow feared that the past few days had indeed been a fantasy and nothing else. Her heart was sure that Harlow's truth was that which they shared in their intimate moments, but surely she couldn't deny this queen before her, her magic or the whispers of her mirrors. She could trust, though, in Harlow and in herself, and with Harlow's hand in hers, she chose to do so.

Nonetheless, Snow breathed better the moment she stepped down from the carriage, the humid scent of rain in the air welcoming her into the world. It smelled of mud as well, but also of wet tree trunks and the busy activity of the town's center, where a small market offered fabrics, vegetables, meat and plenty more. They were met with curiosity despite Harlow's guard arriving earlier to announce them, and as Harlow partook in quick goodbyes to the men that would follow on to the rest of the kingdom with the supplies, a small crowd of onlookers gathered around their party. Snow heard the whispers and knew them to be surprised. Hoping to keep them away from being unkind, she stepped close to Harlow, found her arm and linked it with hers, making her position clear.

"Hoping to make a statement, dear?" Harlow wondered, looking at her for the first time since they'd left the palace. She looked tired and nervous, but her gaze wasn't uncaring.

Snow nodded and let Harlow's obvious provocation go. She felt strange, out and about with Harlow by her side and without a battlefield before her. She looked about herself slowly, watching as Harlow's men distributed wool and wineskins, thick, dark breads and mountains of butter, candles and barrels of apples. She looked upon those last, the red skin beautiful, even tempting, yet the memories they brought back painful.

Snow thought of the war, of the coppery scent of freshly spilled blood upon a battlefield, and hated herself for allowing things to go so far. The people around her feared Harlow so, yet she was to blame for their misery as well, for she had wished for retribution and her desire had been executed by her husband's firm hand. Her husband, who was now somewhere in this kingdom and ready to rescue her from illusory peril.

Turning towards Harlow, she murmured, "Would it that we might have stopped this sooner."

"I started it," Harlow declared, her tone low and only for Snow's ears. Snow wanted to protest the statement, but something in Harlow's steady gaze made her stop. "I shall finish it, as well."

"How ominous you sound, *cariño.*"

Harlow didn't reply, but she reached out for Snow's hand and twined their finger together. They were wearing gloves and Snow felt the touch insufficient. There was so much sentiment that she wanted to express, and it was always easier to convince Harlow of her truths when clothes had been shed and they were standing without the pomp and fair of their regal personas.

Wishing her grim thoughts away, Snow turned to the villagers still peering curiously at them, and walked to them, pulling Harlow with her despite an obvious protest. Harlow was uncomfortable, unused to people other than her court, but her haughty attitude would do her no good. She was a witch, and she could certainly be evil, but there was more to her than the deathly queen she had been made to be. People needed to see beyond her harsh exterior, beyond her otherworldly beauty and the awkward tension painting her eyes and making her movements stiff. Moreover, Harlow needed to give herself to them without the protection of battle armor and magic, so that they could let go of their fear.

Snow had always been naturally inclined towards people, and she enjoyed playing up her part of ditzy princess, whistling when a little girl asked if she could truly talk to birds, offering her hand to be held and candidly trying to offer comfort. It was easy and useless in practical terms, but if she'd learned something as Charles' princess, then that was that people liked getting close to her, liked her warmth and her smile and her sweet disposition. She too had learned that people should be listened to, perhaps more than court members and royal advisors. After all, Harlow had the ears and hearts of her court, yet the people feared her enough that her downfall had begun with them. This war had started as a popular revolt, even if it had been royalty that had executed it.

Harlow remained far from the onlookers, having given up on holding Snow's hand and making herself busy instead with keeping order among her soldiers. Snow looked at her as she moved, graceful and secure in her position of ruler as she didn't know how to be around the villagers. She thought of her as she'd been in that rainy battlefield weeks before, cocky and alluring, calling to her with promises that she hadn't quite understood. War had suited Harlow far more than it had ever suited Snow, but their paths had been intertwined then and they remained so now.

"Princess, are you bewitched?" a voice piped suddenly, pulling Snow's attention to its owner, a little girl that had escaped her mother's arms and was now by Snow's side, her eyes bright and her face dirty, as if she'd been playing in the mud.

Snow smiled, crouching down to girl's height and comforting her mother, who was fussing and apologizing as if she feared her wrath over the girl's impertinence. Snow thought she was a beautiful child, and she would never want her people to ever be afraid of speaking to her, never mind how impolite their ways.

"Do you think I am bewitched?" she wondered, cocking her head to the side to amuse the girl before her and hopefully get her to smile.

The girl did smile, her toothy grin wide, two missing front teeth furthering her charm. "Aren't you afraid of the queen? Did she put you under a spell to do as she says?"

Snow laughed at the child's brazen mouth and at her mother's embarrassed spluttering, and then reassured them both of her good will by pressing a soft caress to the girl's cheek, and even cleaning away some of the dirt from her skin.

"The queen has no need for bewitchment, for I have always loved her."

"You have?"

Snow looked upon Harlow some feet away, and said, "Yes; I once held her hand and wished for us to be friends, and I have loved her dearly ever since."

The girl scrunched her nose exaggeratedly now, showing something like disapproval, or maybe simple confusion. She wasn't the only one, however, if the rest of the villagers around her weren't quite as expressive in their curiosity. Snow and the questioning little girl had gathered an audience of onlookers, and perhaps Harlow's advisors had been right when they'd said that Harlow's shows of good faith would have to begin with Snow's.

"But she's the Evil Queen!"

Snow smiled candidly, the girl's ingenious behavior towards her endearing. Snow had no wish to correct her notions and knew that all change would be slow and painful. Nonetheless, Snow would gladly reassure her of her love towards Harlow, and would hope that to be enough. She parted her lips to speak, but stopped short when she felt a cold raindrop on her head, quickly followed by a second one touching her skin and dripping down the back of her neck, making her shiver. She looked up to see a thin shower of rain begin to fall. It was soft against her face, barely noticeable yet making her short hair feel frizzy, and caressing her in cold pinpricks. Snow stood up and saw the people start looking for shelter. She took a step closer to Harlow and saw her do the same, their gazes meeting across the rain. Harlow's eyes were shiny, almost hypnotizing, and Snow felt her ears buzzing uncomfortably, an omen settling above her head and making her tense up even if unsure of the reason.

Snow reached out but stopped short of moving further, so that her hand was left dangling in the air, cold rain finding the cracks within her clothing and touching the thin skin of her wrist. She looked at it, dumbfounded, and saw the reddish marks of Harlow's love upon her flesh, the color striking against the white fur of her coat and gloves. She felt dizzy, captivated by her own skin and by the strange spell in the air. She breathed in, looking to ground herself, and looked up at Harlow yet again only to find her looking away, up and forward at where a commotion had started to brew.

New sounds broke Snow's trance suddenly, the clash of swords substituting the quiet sounds of the town's market. She searched for the noise, and soon saw a battalion of at least a hundred men trod through the village's main street, swords out and feet quick on the mud, the heavy step of their boots and the clinking of their armor accompanying their battle cry. And at the head of the battalion, there was Charles.

Snow had little time to think, and all she did was step back and closer to Harlow. Harlow's men surrounded them, weapons at the ready and stances wide and tense. There were few of them, however, not nearly enough to face the battalion running their way. Snow yelled Charles' name, but her voice was lost under the chaos brought on by the soldiers.

"Harlow," she called instead, searching for her and finding her arm, clinging to her for dear life and once again trying to find her gaze.

Harlow was looking before her at Charles and his men, however, at her own soldiers building a wall of protection around them. Her eyes were hard and her look sharp, and Snow realized that she was this war's most powerful weapon, never mind how many men Charles had to bring before her. Snow wondered at Harlow's true powers, and remembered that only a few days before she had seen her cast the elements against her enemies through the powers of her mirrors. Could she repeat such a feat? Was the thin rain falling upon them but a reflection of Harlow's own tempest?

There was little time to think or ponder such matters, for soon Charles and his battalion were coming to a stop before Harlow's men. They were breathless but they looked fierce, chaos personified as villagers run towards protection and away from them, hiding behind posts and tents and huddled close together, keeping an eye out for the outcome of the battle brought to the front of their houses. Snow's heart began beating hard inside her chest, going out to the people but having no hope of ever reassuring them. She'd seen whole villages burnt to the ground in the name of their advancement in this war, and she knew Charles wouldn't stop if harsh action was necessary. Would Harlow, though, when Charles had once more betrayed their pact and made his way further into the kingdom?

"Lower your weapons, witch!" Charles bellowed, pulling his visor up so that his eyes were uncovered.

He looked crazed, and Snow knew he was suffering from sleeplessness. He could be obsessive when pushing towards his goals, and without his mother to calm his temper down and only the encouragement of his generals to keep him going, it was evident to Snow that he was at his most manic.

"Lower your weapons!"

His repetition was met with an impasse, Harlow's soldiers keeping their swords up and Harlow's gaze sharply settled on Charles' figure. Snow squeezed her arm where she was holding it, silently begging for a solution that didn't spill any blood.

"Lower you wea–"

"Quiet!" Harlow clamored back, her voice booming and impressive, the edges of her tone brimming with magic.

Charles said nothing else, and it seemed to Snow that the whole village breathed in sync, waiting for the inevitable. Harlow stepped forward, and the circle of her soldiers opened for her to walk past them, her heavy coat trailing behind her and through the mud, her head held high and her gait that of a queen. The jewels upon her tiara shined bright against the grey backdrop of the rainy morning, and as she walked towards Charles and away from Snow, she took on the mantel of Evil Queen and left behind the tentative awkwardness that had conquered her before. She became a creature of legend as she walked, and Snow reached out for her, wishing to pull her back, or to be allowed to walk next to her.

Harlow stood before Charles, no weapon but her own pride to face his steel. She was a queen then, powerful and beautiful and everything Snow wanted.

"Let us have peace, prince," Harlow intoned, surprising her audience with a graceful open gesture of her hands, and a sweet tone to her voice. Snow knew there was venom at the tip of Harlow's tongue, and it stung in her next few words, "Do lower your weapons and let the prince reunite with his long-lost bride; let it not be said that the Evil Queen stands in the path of true love."

Harlow's soldiers answered her order immediately, dropping their stances and hiding their swords in their scabbards. Charles took a moment longer to react, perhaps expecting a betrayal, never mind that he'd been the one to break their pact, and that Harlow had been truthful to her promises. As soon as he felt comfortable, he released himself from his helmet and ran past Harlow and her men, and straight into Snow's arms.

"My wife," he exclaimed, putting his arms around her and lifting her up from the ground in one swift movement.

Snow gasped and held on to his shoulders, looking to steady herself and hating that her feet were no longer on the ground. She had always felt so light within Charles' arms. He smelled of sweat and grime, war clinging to his skin and his scent unpleasantly, and he was still holding his sword, so that Snow could feel the steel at her back, as solid as his arms.

"Charles, please put me down."

He complied, and Snow felt better as soon as her feet touched the ground, her boots sinking in the mud and granting her steadiness. She pushed back to keep Charles from hiding his face, and looked up into his eyes, saying nothing.

“My princess, my magical princess,” he intoned, his voice rough yet tender.

Snow smiled tepidly, guilt sudden and pounding against her chest, the sight of him painful and bittersweet. She was ever so glad that he was alive and seemed well, tired from battle but mostly unharmed. Nonetheless, she had no wish to be his wife, nor his magical princess, just as she had no wish for him to be her hero anymore.

Looking over Charles’ shoulder, Snow saw Harlow’s figure, now far away and blurry, so still that Snow would have sworn she was lifeless.

“Are you well? What has the witch done to you?”

“Nothing! I wrote to you, I implored you to keep away.”

“You must have been bewitched, surely.”

“Oh, dear Charles, I am unharmed, as I promised. Harlow hasn’t been unkind and neither has the court; I have enjoyed visiting my home.”

“Your home is with me, not by that witch’s side! You must be under her spell!”

“Listen to me, for once!” Snow yelled, dropping her arms away from Charles’s shoulders in frustration.

He was ever so involved in his own fantasy of a valiant rescue the he wouldn’t stop to ponder her wishes; she’d known him to be impulsive, and had no doubt that it had been such impetus that had driven him to marry her in the first place.

He turned back from her, dismissing her in favor of facing his enemy, "If the witch is as kind as you speak, then she will agree to your immediate release and will accept her defeat!"

Harlow laughed at Charles' demands, now walking back to them in slow steps, enjoying the eyes that followed her figure. Battle suited her well.

"My defeat?" she questioned, tilting her head as if an amused cat looking at a particularly dumb human.

"I have breached your defenses and stand before you with a fierce battalion! Your men won't win this battle!"

Harlow hummed, thoughtful yet diverted and said, "Perhaps they won't, but you'll do well to mind your real enemy, prince."

Charles moved quickly, minding the obvious threat in Harlow's words, his stance tensing with practiced ease and his sword coming up, his second arm covering his face in lieu of a shield. Harlow was a contrast in languidness, her hand coming up slowly. She had taken off her glove, and she made a show of presenting her palm up to Charles, claiming his attention with her deliberate performance. Harlow cast soft magic over her own skin, a beautiful, ethereal blue flame floating inside her palm. There were gasps around them, maybe even a scream, but Snow only managed to part her lips silently, the magic Harlow was casting unthreatening and only for her own pleasure. The fire in Harlow's hand crawled upon Snow's skin wickedly, pinpricks of feeling burning up her thighs and down her belly, pooling warm as bourbon between her legs. Snow rubbed her thighs together unwittingly, holding in the feeling but not managing to hold in her moan. She stumbled back, embarrassed, but Harlow reached out for her and held on to her arm, extinguishing the magic as she did so.

"What did you do, witch?"

"Just a little trick, prince, but do be wary of who it is that you're facing with your silly sword and your smug, royal look."

"Please…" Snow whined, fastening her hold on Harlow and grabbing at her arm, her shoulder, finding solace in a half embrace.

Harlow's magic was gone, but the effects of her spell remained, pulsing now steadily in Snow's lower belly and keeping her skin abuzz with sensation.

"Easy, princess," Harlow cooed, touching her naked hand to Snow's flushed cheeks, her cold fingers a balm to Snow's senses. She smiled sweetly at Snow, unapologetic but tender, and then let the pad of her fingers draw a soft caress from her cheek and down to her neck, perhaps a promise to make up for her teasing sorcery.

"I demand–"

"You demand nothing, Prince Charles, yet I shall give," Harlow stated, one hand steady on Snow's neck, possessive, and one motioning about herself at the village around her, her kingdom. "There are three days left to our truce; you and your men shall be my honored guests until then." Then, making her voice louder and speaking towards whoever might listen, "And then this war shall be over!"

"I shan't ever–"

"Charles, please, let us rest," Snow pleaded. "Let us rest from this war, let your men rest, your people rest."

Snow's pleas didn't fall on deaf ears, Charles' pride willing to concede in the name of his wife's desire and the comfort of his soldiers. They had been through hell and back; many of them were wounded, and they were all hungry and in need of proper sleep. Charles had always been a good commander to his armies, holding his soldiers in high regard.

The journey back to the palace was a point of discomfort, Charles and Harlow facing each other until Snow broke their standstill and chose Harlow's carriage for a ride back, and not the rump of Charles' stallion. She climbed into the cramped space and felt immediately relieved – she was wet and cold from the rain, and the strokes from Harlow's spell still caressed her tantalizing, bringing a soft quiver to her legs.

Harlow climbed into the carriage quickly as well, and as soon as she gave the order, it started its rickety trot back towards the palace.

"What did you do?" Snow questioned as soon as they were alone. Her tone was forceful, yet Snow could hardly guess at what she was truly asking, whether about her husband being invited to the palace, or the magic Harlow had conjured to make her weak in the knees.

Harlow didn't answer, and whatever anger Snow had gathered died the moment Harlow kissed her, open-mouthed and messy, passion in her lips, her tongue, her spit.

"Oh, please, what did you do to me?"

"A little trick, didn't you like it?" Harlow whispered into her parted lips, her eyes hooded and wanton and her hands fighting Snow's gown and coat, looking for the skin of her thighs and the wet flesh of her pussy.

Snow yielded to the attention, gathering her skirts up and laying down uncomfortably on the small, plushy seat, moaning when Harlow's fingers found her and pounded inside her fast, pulling the strings of her desire and forcefully bringing her to pleasure.

"You were so cruel," Snow whined even as she held Harlow close, her nails finding purchase in Harlow's puffy sleeves. "You were ever so cruel to let him embrace me, to let him join us at the palace."

"Would you rather I finished this war with his blood on my hands? I did it for you."

Snow huffed, closing her thighs around Harlow's wrist and keeping her fingers inside her even after she'd climaxed, wishing for this strange closeness to never end. Uncertainty and decisions waited for her back at the palace, and with guilt, lust and love clouding all her senses, she couldn't be sure she would do right by her heart, or by the kingdom.

"You couldn't help yourself from this little performance, could you?" Snow wondered, her breathing now back to normal and her hand reaching for Harlow's face.

Harlow pouted, playing up the part of whiny child to hide the vulnerability in her voice when she said, "I can't stop you from running to your husband, but I can certainly play my cards."

"I didn't run to him, you sent him my way."

"He's your–"

"Husband and prince, I know. Do not think I am free of guilt, for I have been ever so unkind to him, so unfair and so cruel, but I won't allow you these games, Harlow, not anymore. You said I should choose and I have; surely you know I choose you, but you must promise to be kind."

"I shall do as I please, dear Snow," she replied, pouty still and denying Snow further protests with her lips, her kisses as fiery as before.

They kissed for as long as the journey lasted, their connection languid yet passionate. Snow clung to the feeling, fearing the arrival at the palace, and Harlow and Charles both.

Charles and his men were ushered inside, and while Harlow's generals were ordered to care for the soldiers, Charles was left in Snow's hands. She denied him intimacy and instead had a bath drawn for him. She bid him rest and sleep before dinner. Then, she excused herself and run up the northern tower and to her mother's old rooms, to the window that showed her the cloudy skies and the comfort she'd known as a child. Perched by the window, warm under a heavy blanket and with the sweet scent of rain surrounding her, she looked for her peace, and found that she had none. Guilt weighted heavily on her, as did worry for the future. Charles would never accept her decision to remain with Harlow, she was sure now, yet she couldn't be sure Harlow herself would accept it either.

Dinner was an uncomfortable affair, if Lord Manderly did try to amuse their company with his ever-engaging boar story. Harlow even laughed, big and false and tense, her quiet grace lost in her lie. Snow was anxious throughout as well, seated in between Harlow and Charles and missing the casual touch of Harlow's hand on her arm, and her insistence that she drink more wine. They had built such familiar ease in a short time, and that she had nothing like it to share with Charles was a painful telltale. Charles himself didn't seem preoccupied by such thoughts, busy eating like a starved man and nodding along to stories from his army generals. It wasn't an unusual sight for Snow, but only now did she realize how little they had spoken during meals. She felt rootless, stuck in between a husband she barely knew and a lover of boundless depth and secret.

After dinner, when Charles loudly demanded to have his wife by his side for the night, Harlow put on a queenly performance of acquiescence and left the decision in Snow's hands. Under the scrutiny of the court and before the demanding nature of Charles' request, Snow agreed to a warm goodnight if nothing else.

Alone in a room with Charles, Snow couldn't help but think back to her first night at the palace, when Harlow had laughed during dinner, and touched her hand, and quietly seduced her into her chambers. She had felt like a nervous bride, wild with anticipation, and had fallen into Harlow's embrace without regret. Now, she felt anxious for a completely different reason, and Charles himself didn't seem particularly inclined to seduce her.

"We must be prepared," he said, his stance that of a soldier as he stood by the fire. He'd been bathed and richly dressed, and he cut a most valiant figure.

Snow nodded, not quite knowing what he meant by his words, and fanned herself. The room was stuffy, and she wished Charles hadn't closed all the windows.

"I must plan to storm the palace soon; I must send a message to rest of my troops. You have the servants' ears, you will be our messenger."

"What?" Snow replied. She was dizzy with guilt, and her husband kept speaking of war and strategy. "Why would you storm the palace? Harlow's dea–"

"It's funny that you should speak of the Evil Queen with such familiarity."

"We were close before the war; do not be unfair, Charles."

"Yet she wanted you gone," Charles countered, finally looking up and at her. "I saved you, I went to war for you."

"I know–I know I should be grateful for… but this war has gone on for so long, and Harlow promised a way out."

"Do you believe her pact? That she will vanish once you choose me?"

“I–I do.”

Charles huffed at her answer and pointed out her hesitation, believing it to be doubt over Harlow’s promise. She didn’t dare confess that her apprehension was hiding her contrary desire to stay by Harlow’s side. She was ever so sure Harlow would respect their deal, never mind the outcome, but would Charles? Would he acquiesce to her leaving him; would he relinquish his desire for Harlow’s kingdom?

“We shall speak in the morning when you’re better rested. Let’s sleep.”

Snow shook her head at the request, smiling uncomfortably and hugging her arms about her middle, closed off to Charles’ offer.

“I rather keep to my own rooms.”

After a moment, Charles replied, “As you wish.” He bowed, his posture easy and his movement fluid, politely saying his goodnight.

Snow left his chambers in long steps, lifting her skirts up to allow for a quicker pace. She was shaken and uncomfortable, and she realized that she had never been at ease when alone with Charles. She'd always looked at him as one might the character of a story, the brave prince that had come to her rescue. He belonged in a tale of adventure and gallantry, and she’d never been his match in that regard. Careless, ditzy and without a taste for royal pomp, she had never been the princess in his story. The war had made them partners in crime, however, their mismatched personalities a second thought when they were too busy out in the battlefield.

At the foot of the stairs, Snow stopped to ponder whether she truly wanted to be alone, or whether she wished for Harlow’s company. It took no time at all to begin her climb up the southern tower to Harlow's chambers, and halfway there, she broke into a run, wanting to exert herself. The guards by the double doors didn't stop her and she crossed them in a hurry, safeguarding herself in the strange haven of mirrors and wonder that was Harlow's room.

She found Harlow still dressed and sitting by the window, her eyes drawn to picture of her mother and aunt on the wall, rather than the sky outside. Her copper hair had been let loose, and she'd rid herself of her heavy collar and her tiara; she looked soft in the moonlight.

"I asked you not to play games!" Snow exclaimed upon first seeing her, crazed by the notion of Charles sleeping somewhere in this palace, plotting to take over and keep this war going.

Harlow moved her eyes to her and then reached out, her palm up, silently asking for Snow to come to her.

"What would you have me do, dear Snow?" she wondered. "Claim you for myself before your husband's eyes? Do not think it gives me any pleasure to leave you in his arms."

"I didn't let him hold me," Snow said, timid, as if a confession. "I do not believe he very much wanted to, in any case."

Snow walked towards Harlow's offered hand, grasping at it and letting her frame relax, her shoulders sag and her arms go lax. She pressed a smattering of kisses to Harlow's face, happy to be welcomed. She kissed her nose, her brow, the corner of her lips, the pretty lines at the edge of her eyes. Eventually, she moved to rest between Harlow's arms, her back to Harlow's chest and their limbs locked together, faces pressed close so their cheeks were touching sweetly. She took a moment to look at the painting of

Harlow's mother and aunt, the anger and the sadness present in both of them, and then turned her eyes towards the moon outside.

"Harlow, what will happen in three days?" she wondered, keeping her voice a whisper, wanting to soak in the feeling of their togetherness.

Harlow remained quiet for a time, and Snow had already given up on ever getting and answer when she began to speak.

"I already spoke to you of the blood moon, of the prophecy, of the sacrifice."

"What kind of sacrifice?"

"My mother paid for her revenge in blood, and her promise wrote our fate with it; it is time for her feud to be over," Harlow explained, the obscurity of her words speaking of omens and magic, and of nothing Snow could understand.

"I believed her feud to be over," she argued. "The king's death should have sealed her vengeance, shouldn't it?"

"Yet his blood runs through your veins, as my mother's runs through mine."

The hairs on Snow's arms raised at Harlow's words, her ears ringing with the giggling song of magic in the air. They weren't alone, and the fae were laughing at her, or maybe at Harlow, playing their tricks around silly humans, demanding their flesh and their soul. She turned around in Harlow's arms and searched for her eyes. Harlow's gaze was sad, her eyes puffy and red, filled with grief.

"*Cariño...*"

Harlow shushed her with a kiss, closed-mouthed and pressed hard to Snow's mouth, more a reassurance that a caress. She broke away and cupped Snow's cheeks in her palms.

"I promise no harm shall come to you," she said. "I won't ever hurt you, not ever again; I cannot bear the thought that I once did, that my desires ran so dark, that I–"

"Yet you speak of blood."

"It does paint our destiny."

"You're speaking in riddles," Snow accused. "And the fairies are laughing in my ears."

Harlow shook her head and kissed her again. Snow held on, closing her eyes to the sensation of Harlow's soft skin, parting her lips to invite her in and soothe her grief with the intimacy of their mouths. She spoke no further, and neither did Harlow, and as they came together once more, the ringing laughter of the fae stopped, allowing them rest.

Days of grievance followed, the hours running by Snow as she wished them to slow down, stop time forever and never take her to the deadline of their pact. A blood moon, Harlow had said, and as she'd spoken of sacrifice, Snow had shivered. She couldn't wrap her mind around the meaning of Harlow's words, but she was certain they were an omen of tragedy – Harlow didn't intend to stay with her, and she didn't intend to give her a choice on the matter, either.

Harlow spent the passing hours in her mirror room, locked behind heavy doors and guarded by soldiers. Snow paced the closed doors with worry guiding every step and clogging every thought. She wasn't alone, for Charles too kept a close watch over the place, his plans of treason thwarted by the heavily armed guard Harlow had ordered follow his every step. Unable to plan his attack and sure of Harlow's wicked treachery, he grew angry and frustrated and refused to see reason beyond his own righteous demands for justice. Moreover, his anger built towards Snow, whom he believed either bewitched or foolish, but either way under Harlow's influence.

"You would put your heart in her hands if she asked," he accused. "I saved you when you never wanted it in the first place; burn with her if you'd like, and I will never again call you *wife*."

Guilt buried a small hole within Snow's insides, yet it remained unimportant when uncertainty clawed at her with a vicious grip. She couldn't hope to deny Charles' words, however hateful, and she didn't have it in her to blame him for them when only a few weeks had been enough to dispel her of notions of loving him. They had lived together for years as husband and wife, yet one single look from Harlow had undone Snow from the insides, calling at her pounding heart and pulling her towards the edge as a siren might call a doomed sailor.

If Harlow denied her the daylight, then the night she offered as a gift. Once the sun set and darkness began casting shadows about the palace, Snow was welcomed within the recesses of Harlow's tower, inside her embrace and her bed. Words were few and far between, and lovemaking became an exercise in desperation as they clung to each other. Snow welcomed each morning with new scratches and bruises, and knew that Harlow's skin would be equally marred. She hoped the shape of her nails and lips engraved upon Harlow's skin would grant Harlow comfort, if not hope.

Upon the third day of their madness, Snow left her spot by the double doors of the mirror room and climbed the stairs up Harlow's tower instead. She walked into Harlow's chambers, covered every mirror and undressed carelessly, dropping coat, gown, corset and shoes on the floor. She climbed into Harlow's bed in the comfort of her shift, and after letting her eyes linger upon the painting by the bed for a brief moment, she closed her eyes tight, wishing for reprieve. As sleep refused to claim her, she cursed Harlow's mother for raising her for revenge; she cursed her father, the king, for his cruelty and his evilness, for the path of destruction he was still carving, even from beyond the grave; she cursed Charles for his wish for war and conquest; she cursed herself for her weakness and her anger; she cursed Harlow for giving into her darkest desires and daring to destroy that which she loved in the name of fate; and she cursed the fairy folk for playing with puny humans, for finding amusement in their grief. Then, she forgave them all, for they were all to blame and none of them flawless, if governed by strange desires.

It was in her hands to put an end to their circle of blood, hers and Harlow's, and with that thought in mind and her eyes closed painfully tight, she fell asleep.

Snow woke up to a whispered lullaby. Sleep clung to her senses, and dreams clouded her mind, yet the otherworldly song pulled her from her comfortable slumber, threads of consciousness painful as prickles as she opened her eyes. Her eyes felt stuck together. She forced them open in heavy blinks, sound and sight breaking past her stupor and taste following soon behind, the pasty flavor of her mouth uncomfortable against her lips and tongue. Smell was kinder, the soft night breeze bringing with it the scent of spring, as uncanny as the ringing song in her ears, the mixed perfume of lilies, roses and marigolds cutting through the wintry air.

Awoken from her slumber, Snow felt her senses sharpen suddenly, the sweet lullaby screeching against the inside of her skull and becoming a shrill warning of danger. She covered her ears, discomforted and abruptly scared, and as the unearthly scream pierced through the last remnants of her dormancy, she looked out the window, breathless. It was indeed nighttime, and if the air was perfumed by the bizarre scent of spring flowers, then the skies shone in alien red hues, a full, blood moon crowning the clear night.

Snow climbed down from the bed thoughtlessly, her feet meeting the cold stone floor and pushing her into a breathless run. Down the stairs she went, holding on to the rails as she stumbled over more than one step a time, her shift flying behind her and her hair jumping up and down around her face. She arrived before the doors of Harlow's mirror room and found them open, a scene of battle before them. Surrounded by guards and with his sword held up threateningly, Charles screamed, revenge and justice both filling his speech.

"What is–what happened?" Snow asked, her tone so thin that no one took notice of her.

Brimming with anxiety, she barreled her way in between Charles and the guards, taking full notice of Harlow's advisors in the scene, as well as many members of the household. Behind her, Charles yelled, his intentions of grabbing at her thwarted by Harlow's men, who held him steady with threatening stances. Snow ignored them all, breathing heavily and looking for answers, and finding them only within Mrs. Agnes' kind and worried eyes. She reached out for her, grabbing at her old hands and feeling them tremble.

"Mrs. Agnes, where is she, where did she go?"

"The forest, child, leaving us the same way she once appeared, dressed in flowers and leaves; what is she going to do?"

Snow didn't stop and think, instead running once more, this time towards the forest, following the invisible trail Harlow had left for her. She run outside as she was, and soon her feet were racing over the wet, cold ground, naked yet fast, forgetting to be in pain. Night air hit her skin, her flushed cheeks, her arms and her legs, her nightshift a translucent cape failing to save her from the winter cold. Nonetheless, she ran, her senses numb and her mind abuzz, the ringing whispers of the fairy folk following her every step, growing fainter and suddenly spiking up, laughing at her as she pursued their mystery.

Remotely, Snow heard her name being called, the wind carrying Charles' voice as he ran behind her. She paid it no mind, breathing heavily against the wintry wind and rushing into the forest, its darkness welcoming her as it had once before. It laughed at her – not the forest but the fae that lived within it. They were playing with her, guiding her steps but denying her otherwise, keeping her destination hidden.

Abruptly, she came to stop. She had crossed the limits of the forest, run past the sweet stone bridge over the river, through the thick trees and all the way into her favored clearing. There, her steps failed her and she fell to the ground, her hands burning up in pain when they touched the crusty dirt. She cried out. Hoping to hold herself together, she stayed kneeling on the ground, her arms around her frame as cold seeped through her skin, naked but for her thin, useless shift. She felt the sudden need to do away with it, too, to make herself a creature of this forest that she loved and hated both.

She looked about herself, madness clinging to the edges of her mind, and saw nothing but shadows painted red. She had run through this forest once before in a panic, and only pain had followed. She refused to repeat such pattern, to allow this terrible magic to rule her life.

"Guide me to the grove!" she exclaimed to the wind, hoping her voice carried. "If you do indeed favor her, if your prophecy makes her queen, guide me to her!"

The fairy song quieted then, and the forest was suddenly eerily quiet, only the creatures of the night daring to fill the silence. An owl hooted, and following its angry call, Snow heard Charles' voice, calling for her. She breathed once, twice, and her prince was suddenly stumbling his way into the clearing, rushed and careless, his steel in his hand.

"Snow!"

"Quiet, please!" she requested. "Please, let me listen to the wind."

He yelled again, yet over his voice Snow heard giggled laughter, a chorus of singing voices, of butterflies taking flight. She closed her eyes, ignored Charles, and felt her feet moving to the magical sound of otherworldly whispers. She murmured her thankfulness to the wind and stood up. She moved slowly, her rushed pace now dancing steps, following the music of magic and spells. She breathed as the fae laughed against her ear, mocking if helpful, loving and hateful at the same time, bringing her to uncertain destiny. Yet Snow danced with them, around them, their song of old a willing partner.

Snow danced her way through the bushes and trees and into the flowery pathways of Harlow's grove. Strange, bright flowers welcomed her, shining bright yellows and blues against the red darkness of the moonlight, painting a spellbinding route for her to follow.

"Fairy lights," she murmured, and laughed when the fae giggled at her silly notions.

Cottoned by their song and dance Snow made her way into the grove, where the sweet sound of falling water awoke her to her surroundings. The grove wasn't warm today, and the only light was that of the moon, which glinted in ghostly pale blues and spectral dark reds over the moving water. The wind blew, soft, whistling a chorus of voices and shaking the tree leaves and the grass. It was cold. Moreover, Snow felt frightened, and she hugged her arms once she finally stopped moving.

"Snow!" Charles screamed behind her.

He had followed her into the grove, and she couldn't fathom why the fairy folk had allowed him here when this place was meant only for their favored. It must have been true what Harlow had said, that the veil was thinner by the red moon, that their world wasn't quite theirs when magic floated under the shadows of the blood night.

"You shouldn't have come here," she said, feeling suddenly calm when faced with Charles' strain.

Snow walked further into the grove, willfully ignoring Charles and looking instead at Harlow, who was so lost in herself that she had failed to take notice of them.

Harlow was kneeling by the edge of the water, naked, beautiful, a nymph inhabiting her magic abode. The flowers painted on her body shone bright on her tan skin, and her hair, dark copper, shone radiant as if it was the sun hitting it, and not this doomed moonlight. The dagger she held in her hand had a hard glint to it as well, the blade that Harlow had trained upon her own stomach radiantly silver.

"*Cariño,*" Snow called.

Harlow turned to her, her movements slow as if spellbound. Her eyes caught Snow's, a beacon of light in the darkness, if clouded with grief.

"You shouldn't have come here," Harlow told her, dismissing her as Snow herself had dismissed Charles not moments ago.

Snow shook her head, denying her human nature, claiming for herself a place in this world of magic. She belonged here because she belonged with Harlow, because their blood was tied by a terrible destiny.

"But I did," she replied. "I did, because you gave me a choice, Harlow. You said the future was mine to decide upon, and you cannot deny me now, not after everything."

"It was a ploy, surely you know."

"But why?"

Harlow said nothing, and Snow walked closer towards her, her steps slow as if approaching a scared animal. Emotion clogged her throat as time passed, as Harlow remained still and Charles complained behind her, both of them holding a blade in their hands. Snow felt tears in her eyes and let them fall, let them trace warm pathways down her cheeks, carve her feelings into her skin.

"Why?" she repeated. "Why bring me here, why keep me close?"

The dagger fell to the ground when Harlow reached out, and Snow met her immediately, holding her hands and taking in her penitent position. Harlow looked up, tears in her eyes, and kissed their joined fingers, the knuckles of Snow's hands. Her lips were as soft as a whisper, so that Snow felt herself victim of an illusion, a cruel mockery of the singing fairies. It was Harlow before her, nonetheless, frail and small as she'd never seen her before.

"I wished for redemption, for forgiveness," Harlow said, her voice raspy and slow, a confession parting her lips painfully. "And I may not deserve it, but my darling, I am selfish even at the end."

"At the end?"

"Blood has to seal my mother's promise of revenge, and I won't spill yours, not when I have hurt you so in the past, when I promised myself that I would never again fall under the spell of my own darkness. Let it be me that ends this once and for all."

"And strip me of decision yet again?" Snow exclaimed, holding forcefully to Harlow's hands when she made to move away, perhaps to grasp at the blade again. "Forget about the fairies and fate, forget about blood moons, Harlow! Fight your way through this with me," she pleaded.

Harlow shook her head, and Snow noticed for the first time that she was manic, that her eyes failed to settle but when she was looking into Snow's. How long had the fae been singing in her ears? Had she been driven mad?

"Harlow–"

"To risk it all again, I couldn't."

"Har–"

Snow interrupted herself when Harlow pulled at her hands and freed herself, immediately grasping at the dagger. She stood up on weak legs, stumbling backwards as she held the dagger up and held it close to her belly yet again.

"No!"

"Let her Snow, let her die if that's what she wants!" Charles bellowed suddenly, his voice cutting through their intimacy and running cold as ice down Snow's spine.

"Don't!" Snow ordered, at him and Harlow both.

"Snow, my darling, let it be, let me–"

"Let her! Quit dithering, witch, and use that blade! Cut your own throat and spare us the guilt!"

"No!" Snow repeated, useless, tired, anxious as she reached forward towards Charles, looking at his sword and at Harlow's dagger.

Harlow lifted the dagger, and though unclear of its destiny, Snow launched herself at it, grasping at Harlow's wrist and cursing when it escaped her grasp. She tried yet again, and she fought Harlow and her most terrible instincts. Charles' demands rang against her ears, dreadful, extreme, impossible. She moved her head this way and that, looking in between them mindlessly, struggling with Harlow and wishing for Charles to stand back, to let this war end as it had started, with only Harlow and herself to battle.

"Enough!" Charles bellowed, instinct taking over and his steel glinting bright red under the moonlight as he thrust it forward, his intent righteously murderous.

"No!" Snow screamed, pressing her body to Harlow's before the sword could touch her, becoming an unwitting shield.

Snow's voice died amidst her screaming, her mouth parted silently as pain burned her back, her stomach, her whole being. Her back arched uncomfortably, bones crumbling under her suddenly impossible weight, and she crumbled to the ground in a pile of awkward limbs, hands like claws and blood flowing under her where Charles' sword had pierced her. She struggled against the pain, coughing up warm blood as her hands dropped heavily by her sides, her back resting against the ground as pain made her shiver. Never before had she felt such agony, feverish ache pooling on her stomach and blinding her to any other sensation.

"What did you do? What did you…"

Voices flowed like water around her, imprecise and foreign. Harlow and Charles were moving above her now, screaming at each other, yet all she could see was the moon above her in the sky, its deep red color mocking her pain. She shook with, feeling herself grow faint.

"No, no! Nonononono…"

Hands settled above her wound, pressing tight so that she cried out in pain.

"This is not your offering… Please… please… If you ever cared, if you ever favored me, if…"

A litany of words surrounded her, Harlow's voice issuing a prayer as she settled her forehead against her hands and above Snow's wound. Snow clung to it, trembling from the pain, feeling herself grow cold and detached, willing numbness to claim her so the pain would go away. She closed her eyes, and as she asked for reprieve, Harlow's voice gave her none, cradling her with its cadence, with its plea.

Snow was cold, though, so very cold, and the fae were laughing at her, giggles like butterflies fighting Harlow's voice, ghostly fingers prickling at her skin and denying her rest. They laughed and laughed and laughed, but as Harlow prayed, her voice conquered the giggles, turned them into a song.

And then, Snow felt a warm burst of sensation on her skin. Harlow's hands felt like balm on her stomach, soft, wonderful, gentle, the touch of her fingers willing the pain away, stroking it away from her body, doing away with it. She must be dying, Snow thought, surely she must be dying and Harlow's softness was but a parting gift. The warmth didn't stop, though, and the pain faded away, the place where her skin had been cut feeling tender but soft, like new skin over an old scar. Snow hummed, content, her limbs loosening up, relaxing against the fresh grass below her, dragging her towards painless slumber. Before dormancy claimed her, she felt the sun warm upon her cheeks, and she smiled.

The sun shone bright still in Harlow's grove, and Snow canted her neck backwards, catching the warm rays on her skin and enjoying the feeling of them against her face, her neck and her chest. She breathed in, feeling her breasts come up and then down. Resting between them, Harlow's hand was steady, firm, as if making sure that she was still there, and that she was still breathing.

Between her legs, Harlow's second hand was moving, however, slow and precise and wonderful, her fingers already so familiar with her pussy that even the thought of them made Snow wet. Today it seemed impossible to her that Harlow should give her more pleasure – they had spent their day frolicking in the water and laying on the grass, and they hadn't stopped touching since the early morning. Surely Snow's body was spent.

"I can't," she whined. "*Cariño,* I'm done."

“A little more…” Harlow countered, humming softly and bringing her mouth to Snow’s neck, finding a spot bruised by her kisses and sucking softly on the tender skin.

Snow moaned breathily, wrapping herself about Harlow and denying any wish to stop. Hands on her hair and legs around her hips, Snow kept Harlow right where she was, fingers inside her, mouth at her neck, taut nipples casually brushing against her own, bellies shivering together. Harlow was sweaty, and she smelled of the grass that had stuck to her hair during their rolling around and of sex, of clammy skin and her own sticky arousal.

“I really don’t think I can,” she repeated, breathless, her voice a murmur of hot air against Harlow’s throat.

“Do you want me to stop?”

“Mmmm, not yet, not yet.”

Harlow laughed, the sound bubbly and clear. She kissed slowly down Snow’s neck, over her flushed collarbones and the soft swell of her breasts, and her fingers grew slower as she traveled her skin, making Snow shiver as she came down from her overstay in the heights of pleasure. She would feel Harlow inside her for hours even after she’d stopped touching her, she was sure, and the thought made her moan again.

Harlow took her time, playing Snow’s body with ease, pulling away and then coming closer again, caressing her as she brought her down. Snow breathed out, eventually spent, and let her shoulders relax against the grass. She blinked her eyes open slowly and looked up at Harlow, perched above her and still straddling her hips, naked and beautiful and free, her hands soft on Snow’s belly.

“We are going to be late,” Snow said after a moment, now looking at the sun up in the sky.

The grove had a funny way of rendering time unimportant.

“One can’t be late to the winter solstice,” Harlow countered. “No one cares about timing when there are bonfires to be had and good wine to spare.”

“Mrs. Agnes would beg to disagree.”

Harlow groaned, playing up her annoyance even as she smiled one of her pretty grins, the gap between her teeth making her allure soft.

“Mrs. Agnes would dare disagree with a queen.”

“Of course! And you let her, too,” Snow said, laughing, feeling giddy still.

They kept quiet, unwilling to leave the grove just yet. Snow stretched her arms above her head, pulling the muscles and feeling the pleasant burn travel down her limbs and to her shoulders. When she rested them back on the ground and by her sides, her fingers absentmindedly caught dust instead of grass. She looked at the place where her hand was resting, where grass no longer grew. It was only a small circle, but it was ugly, and it broke the harmonious balance of the grove, of its sweet water and spring flowers, of the magic of the sun that was bright even during the winter. It was still painted in the dark red hues of her blood.

Harlow moved to grasp at Snow’s hand and move it away from the spot. She took it and brought it to her lips so she could kiss each finger and knuckle softly, her eyes closed and a reverent sigh parting her lips. Snow smiled at the gesture, and let herself feel the plumpness of Harlow’s lips against the tender skin of her hand, instead of thinking of the phantom pain low on her belly.

A year had passed since the night Snow’s blood had coated this grove, sinking into the earth and paying the price of ancient revenge and furious destiny. Harlow had meant to make a sacrifice out of her own life, but Charles’ unfortunate intrusion had changed fate and nearly ended Snow's instead. Harlow had prayed to her fairy folk and her magic had saved Snow, the warmth of her spell closing her wound and breathing life back into her body. A scar remained low on her belly where Charles' sword had pierced it, however, it was hidden under the pinkish white hues of the apple blossom the fae had painted on her skin.

Now, Harlow dropped her hand back on the ground and lowered herself to kiss the petals gracing Snow's skin. Snow giggled, feeling ticklish, and touched her fingers to Harlow's cheek, hoping to offer silent comfort. They didn't speak about that night often, and when they did, their words turned harsh and opened old wounds. They were flawed, after all, in their love and in their own demons, but tonight, Snow hoped Harlow wouldn't brood over the recent past.

"Lay down with me," Snow requested.

Harlow did as she was told, falling by Snow's side and making a pillow out of her arm, so that she could remain close and still caress the petals painted on Snow's skin. Snow did the same, letting her own hand linger on the lilies traveling down Harlow's thigh.

Once upon a time, Snow had woken up from a terrible slumber to Charles' handsome face. Not by true love's kiss, as many stories still liked to tell, but because he'd dislodged the poisoned apple from her throat when moving her. She had awoken from her second sleep by Harlow's side, her skin healed and tears in her eyes, warmth seeping through her. They had held hands under the sun of the grove, the blood moon no longer crowning the sky. It had been an ending and a beginning both, and one that Snow had refused to forsake.

It hadn't been easy, not with Charles' anger and a kingdom still aflame with war, not when Harlow herself still thought that her death would have been a better solution. Snow had taken charge of her life this time around, however, and had endeavored to convince Charles to leave things be, to accept that they were never meant to be man and wife, and to retire from this useless war and let the limits between their kingdoms be as they once were. He had conceded in the name of what little love they had shared, and hoping to find redemption from the most terrible instinct that had nearly seen him as her murderer.

The long-armed consequences of war haunted them to this day, however. They had done terrible damage to their kingdoms and their people, but their newfound peace was helping them make strides in the right direction.

Their reputation remained a matter of concern, and one which Harlow still brooded over, even when she'd refurbished her mirror room into a dancing hall, and when Snow made her best efforts to pull her away from her own mind and the shadows behind the looking glass. The fae meant her no harm, but they had no notion of human nature, and Harlow remained attuned to them, and often felt more comfortable among their whispers than surrounded by people. Snow heard them too now, sometimes, at the back of her mind, and the grove was always open to her, so that she knew that terrible blood night had afforded them harmony and favor.

"You're thinking," Harlow said after time, covering the apple blossom with her palm, as if protecting the skin that had been cut. "It's a most terrible habit to develop so late in life, darling."

Snow smiled, smacked Harlow's ass for the cheek in her retort, and laughed at her yelp. Were they not so spent, the slap may have led to something else. Their intimacy had only flourished during the last year; they were openly in love and shameless in their passion. They knew to find each other in caresses and bites, in scratches and kisses, in ropes tied about their wrists and their bodies writhing together, in balancing power, love, happiness and grief on their flesh. They had made Harlow's rooms into their home, and her bed into their church, where they could always find each other despite their sorrows and regrets.

Harlow still brooded, plagued by the darkness that had taken root in her heart, that still plagued her temper. Even if she'd shed her mantel of Evil Queen, terrible desires run in her veins and doubt clouded her thoughts from time to time, prophecies of old telling her that they were living their happiness in borrowed time, and that tragedy was sure to struck. Snow knew such moods would never belong to her, and that part of Harlow would forever be attached to her world of wonder, to the magic she had been born into. Snow had her own grievances to dwell on, the angry and confusing times of her marriage and the war, the resentment that sometimes grasped at her at the thought of Harlow's past treasons and attempts on her life. She still refused to eat apples, even when they had blossomed as beautiful paintings on her skin.

Snow shook such thoughts away, and turned to Harlow instead. "I have been thinking I would love to have mother's old rooms turned into a birdhouse."

"A birdhouse, of all things?"

"A giant, beautiful birdhouse where birds can come and go as they please. The children of the court will love it."

"And they will keep saying that you talk to birds and that you are indeed a witch."

Snow laughed, already knowing what rumors said about her ever since she had chosen to remain by Harlow's side. Either she must be a witch or she must be enchanted and under Harlow's terrible spell – that she may love the queen never seemed to cross anyone's mind.

"A good witch," Snow replied, amused.

Harlow moved to settle her weight on her elbow so she could look down at Snow. Her hair fell over her shoulder, the curtain of deep red curls tickling Snow's side.

"Have a birdhouse if you want one, dear Snow; have whatever you want."

They kissed slowly, Snow's hand on Harlow's cheek and their breaths warm as their tongues touched. When they broke apart, they quit their lingering and lazily stood up, collecting clothes as they went and helping each other to button and lace. It was a familiar scene by now, a ritual of sorts that they used to say goodbye to the place of rest that they had made out of the grove.

Outside its magic doors, there was the world – a world recovering from war, where tongues ran with stories and where legend had begun to build around them. The princess and the Evil Queen, their story that of an apple, an eternal slumber, a prince and a true love's kiss, all of it only a half-truth, and failing to encompass who they were. Moreover, it was a world where Harlow sulked and grew quiet, where she was difficult, where her spell seemed otherworldly and sometimes scary, where she grew awkward when visiting the villagers, where some would forever know her as the Evil Queen. It was also a world where Snow felt guilt weight down on her shoulders, where regret persecuted her thoughts and made her mind her actions, where she was ditzy and sometimes inappropriate, where she didn't completely understand royal duties and where she would forever be judged in terms of her treason.

Nonetheless, it was their world, and now they had a chance to build it together, even outside the confines of this magical safe haven.

Before leaving the grove, Harlow combed Snow's hair, short still and curling sweetly about her cheeks, and then adorned it with a beautiful tiara, a symbol that she too was queen, whether as consort or by right she didn't care, but an equal to Harlow's standing. Snow thought it heavy and much rather preferred pretty satin ribbons, but for tonight she would be a queen, if Harlow wished it so.

They walked hand in hand through the forest, now covered in gowns and furs to protect themselves from the winter. It was a good night nonetheless, not too cold and almost breezeless, so they took their time walking back, steps short and eyes distracted.

"I would always think of the winter solstice when I was away," Snow confessed suddenly, nodding when Harlow hummed questioningly. "I thought about sitting with you by the bonfire and looking up at the stars. We would always sit close together because it was cold, and I thought it was so lovely."

Harlow smiled, squeezing her hand, and then said, "I remember; I loved you best during those nights."

Snow smiled, content, saying nothing and hoping Harlow would continue speaking. Words often failed Harlow when she tried to speak her love, they tumbled awkwardly from her mouth and made her loose her graceful demeanor, as if foreign and uncomfortable. Snow battled such discomfort by proclaiming her own love time and again.

"It's a strange night for me," Harlow continued. "Nature is reborn during the yuletide and the fae sing and dance to celebrate the reawakening; can you hear them?"

"Faintly," Snow replied, only now paying attention to the quiet, olden song at the back of her mind.

"I feel as if I should dance with them. But the court dances tonight as well, and never more than tonight are they creatures of magic and spring… and to have you by my side, so very warm, so quiet and so happy. I couldn't believe that we weren't meant to be together on such nights."

Snow felt each word inside her chest, the easy confession warming up her insides and making her heart pound. They should have known, back then, that this was their true destiny – this togetherness, this love. And if not destiny, then choice, their own and not their parents', or the fae's. Love in which to grow, in which to heal, in which to live. Love to surround them and their kingdom, to cure it of the sins of old, of the cruel king that had started their path with the blood of others, so that they could end it with their own.

They left the forest not long later, and were met by the festivities. Big bonfires had been lighted at the edge of the woods, and wine and food ran freely as music played, villagers and the court alike celebrating together on this special night. Mrs. Agnes received them, and after scolding them for being late and setting a terrible example, she gave them cups filled with warm wine, and instructed them to find something sweet to eat.

Together, they sat on an empty log and looked at the fire. They sat close together, very close, their thighs touching and their hands clasped about each other. When Harlow smiled, funny gap between her teeth and otherworldly beauty, Snow did as well. Together, they looked up at the clear night sky.

To You, The Reader

I greatly appreciate you taking the time to read the story weaved by these words.

Please, if you enjoyed it, leave a small review. One simple line is more than enough!

Thank you,

Lola Andrews

Join Lola's mailing list and receive a FREE short story.
Werewolves. Lesbians. Action and romance.
All mixed together in the fast-paced urban fantasy
Dark Alleys.

Subscribe here: http://eepurl.com/gn-q6j

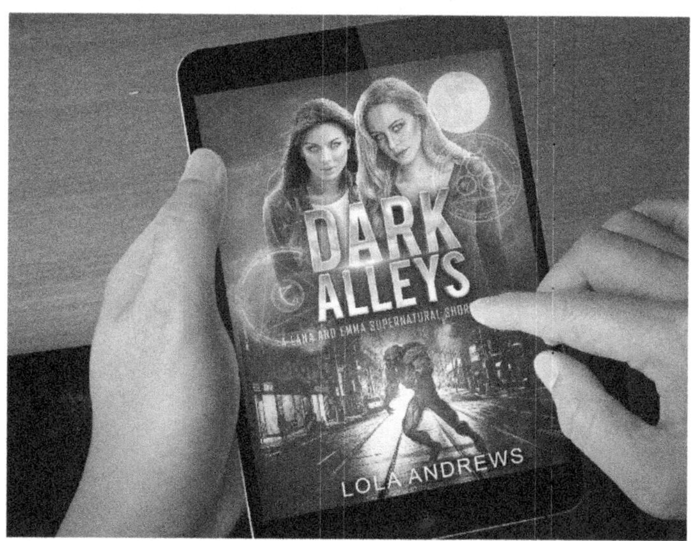

ABOUT THE AUTHOR

Lola Andrews is part-writer, full-time IT consultant and out-of-the-closet nerd. She grew up between Spain and Venezuela, and continues making use of her multicultural upbringing to seem more interesting in conversation. She studied engineering and later worked putting a bunch of numbers in Excel Spreadsheets.

If you like her stories, please feel free to find her on social media, or shoot her a note at 2018.lola.andrews@gmail.com She's always happy to hear from people who have read her work, and answers every email she receives.

If you liked this story, please write a short review on Amazon. Any kind words are greatly appreciated. The number of reviews any book receives greatly improves its chances of doing well on Amazon.

Subscribe to Lola's mailing list here: https://bit.ly/2zzMUCf
Amazon: www.amazon.com/Lola-Andrews/e/B079P89FMP
Twitter: @lola_andrews200
Facebook: https://bit.ly/2Q1feHO

www.lolaandrews.com